THE

PRESIDENT

AND THE

FROG

THE

PRESIDENT

AND THE

FROG

Carolina De Robertis

ALFRED A. KNOPF

NEW YORK

2021

THIS IS A BORZOI BOOK PUBLISHED BY
ALFRED A. KNOPF

www.aaknopf.com

LIBRARY OF CONGRESS CATALOGING-IN-PUBLICATION DATA
Names: De Robertis, Carolina, author.
Title: The president and the frog / Carolina De Robertis.
Description: First Edition. | New York: Alfred A. Knopf, 2021. |
"This is a Borzoi book"—Title page verso.
Identifiers: LCCN 2020028324 | ISBN 9780593318416 (hardcover) |
ISBN 9780593318423 (ebook)
Subjects: GSAFD: Historical fiction.
Classification: LCC PS3604.E129 P74 2021 | DDC 813/.6—dc23
LC record available at https://lccn.loc.gov/2020028324

Jacket design by Alex Merto

Manufactured in the United States of America
First Edition

To each of you who've ever felt despair

amor y ánimo

We live in a marvelous world but we can't always
see its marvels.

JOSÉ MUJICA, FORMER PRESIDENT OF URUGUAY, 2017

DIONYSUS: Go on. Keep croaking. I don't care.
CHORUS OF FROGS: We'll croak on 'til our throats
   wear out.
We'll croak all day.
DIONYSUS: Brekekekex koax koax
You never beat me in this play!
CHORUS OF FROGS: And you've no chance to win
   your way,
not matched with us.

ARISTOPHANES, *THE FROGS*, 405 B.C.

THE

PRESIDENT

AND THE

FROG

O nce upon a time, in a near-forgotten country, on a certain mid-November afternoon, an old man sat at his kitchen table and listened for the world beyond. No cars, not yet, only a breeze rattling the windowpane and the song of a single stubborn thrush. The reporters would be here any moment, with their arms full of equipment and their heads full of questions, looking the way reporters usually did in the old man's house: amazed, disoriented, as if they'd just landed in some unmapped corner of the planet. As if it were some miracle, him in a ramshackle home, as if—and this was the part that tickled him most—*as if he were a normal man.* It was strange, how stunned they were, no matter how thoroughly they'd researched and prepared, no matter how much they already knew about the so-called Poorest President in the World, a man who'd led his country while living in a place, well, like this, could it be true, this house right here, there must be some mistake, they'd pulled up to the wrong gate, it couldn't have been these four walls that he chose over the Presidential Palace, how could anyone run a country from a humble farmhouse at the edge of town, more hut than house by the standards of some of the countries from which they'd flown; why would anyone even attempt to lead from such a place, why for that matter would anyone donate more than half their salary to charity, especially as president. There had to be a reason other than what the public had heard so far. And so they often opened with questions about it, tinged with disbelief as well as an amusing kind of hubris, as if they really thought they were the first to ask, as if by asking they could dig up some truth so buried it had never seen the sun.

A common first question was *why? Why live the way you do?*

There had been so many interviews throughout the presidency, and even now that it was over. He'd thought it would abate once his term ended, but the requests had not let up. He'd had to become more discerning, but still, he wouldn't stop. Not yet. Not until he had to. Because there was so much, always, left to do. He watched a few specks of dust dance in a slant of light, just above the cluttered kitchen counter. So much dust. He'd wiped all the counters this morning—not under all the jars and bottles and cups that congregated exuberantly there, but still, he'd wiped around them, and he'd swept the slightly uneven floorboards, yet here they were again, specks of dust, floating languidly as if time belonged to them.

An engine outside. He approached the front door. Yes, there they were, out at the gate. A van. Two of them this time, a man and a woman, from Germany, or was it Sweden, he couldn't remember now, his calendar was so full they'd all started to bleed together and in any case a welcome to them all. These two seemed young, limber, they were busy disembarking and gathering equipment and hadn't yet seen him in the doorway. The spring air was lovely, the warmest so far, that kind of November sun that flirts with your skin, coy about the summer to come. A good day for an interview in the garden. He'd suggest the garden, politely, but really that was the only place; usually, with two of them and the camera to set up on a stand, there wasn't enough space in the combined kitchen and attached living room, and anyway they were never satisfied by the interior light, no sweeping vistas here, ha, not even close, nothing like the majestic windows and fancy molding in the official Presidential Residence of his own country, or of countries he'd visited as head of state, but despite that or, more accurately, for that very reason, he knew they'd want to see the inside of his house and get their own footage, direct images of—look, can you believe it, breaking news—the way an old man lives, and really, he thought to himself, regardless of what they say that's all you are, an old man.

The reporter said something to the cameraman, then looked up and caught the ex-president's eye. She smiled with genuine pleasure and waved. She was wearing sneakers, no high heels, a sensible and poised woman in her early forties perhaps, older than the cameraman with his broad shoulders and shaggy hair and a look about him like one of those surfer types who seemed to always long for the bobbing waves while she looked more like, say, an elementary school principal, warm and eagle-eyed. There were interviews and then there were interviews, and this reporter, he realized, watching her start up the path toward him, would not be one of the predictable ones who lingered in the shallows. She might not be the kind to start with that common question, the one about the house, the way he lived, that Why. She might start at the end, or in the middle, with the disastrous recent election in North America, a catastrophe only just beginning to send its ripples into the world along with questions surely on the tips of many journalists' tongues, such as *how the hell do we carry on? what will it mean? what now?*—or maybe she'd start all the way back in pre-

historic times, his guerrilla years, his prison years, perhaps that other popular question, which was *how? How
did you survive it and become, well, ehm, you?* A kind of
dive right into deeper waters, she'd be capable of that, the
smart ones often took that route, thinking it gave them
more time to burrow around the ocean floor in search of
secrets to pry open. As if secrets were the pearls inside of
oysters, held in crusty shells and he himself was a crusty
old geezer after all, so why not. They fancied themselves
pearl divers, the kind you read about in other countries
who knifed down and tapped on shell after shell. There
was a name for them, what was it, he couldn't remember,
not the first word to slip his mind this week, damn it, but
what could he do, at least he was still sharp enough for a
lot of things and, in any case, whatever they were called
that was how they did it, the pearl people, tapping with
their fingertips, while reporters went about it with their
questions.

Tap tap, what's in there.

He didn't want to be tapped at anymore, not today,
he thought with a hint of panic, which startled him,
because what did it matter, he knew how to do this, he
could do it in his sleep, and anyway there was nothing
special to be found, was there? What secrets could this
German-or-Swedish-maybe woman walking toward him

be after? What could be left to pry open in him? Surely she knew better than to think she could uncover something new.

He was done with all that.

He'd been baring himself for years now.

He was eighty-two years old, full of creaks and aches and bullet wounds that itched with the turning of the weather. He'd told all his stories and answered all the questions, he had a reputation as a man who loved to talk and it was true, he'd talked and talked throughout these recent years, these presidential years, about the old days, the new days, the yet-to-come-what-will-we-see days, he'd spoken more words than he'd have thought possible in a single lifetime. When he was a little boy, he used to imagine that somewhere in heaven (for this imagining took place in that very early period when he still believed a heaven could exist) a vast crowd of majestic registers counted all the words spoken by every human being in the world, that every time a child was born a new register appeared gleaming among the rows, and all you had to do to see the sum of your life's speech was reach that heaven-place and find the beautiful machine that bore your name, like one of those old-fashioned cash registers that ring cheerily when you feed them or take anything away, only glowing, and instead of showcasing the number of pesos in its little window, it displayed the total of your spoken words. It would spool out every syllable you'd ever uttered on a bright, kilometers-long receipt. Well. If such a place existed, he'd surely have the longest spool of anyone alive. Yes, there were the lonely years of silence, but damn, since then he'd really made up for lost time. What a kick it would be to see the number on his personal word-register in the ether. It amazed him now, his childish faith that the universe would bother to preserve such elaborate records of people's spoken lives. Even if it could, why would it bother? Naturally, he'd learned as he grew up that the opposite was true: most human speech went unrecorded, unregistered, even today in the era of gadgets everywhere to document your sounds, and certainly there was no such thing as what he'd imagined, no gathering of heavenly contraptions, no spooling notes, no system of preservation. If anything, the forces of the world leaned toward erasure. There was nothing except people, their voices, and the air that held them, with time's river sweeping over it all.

Still. Not all speech dissolved. And even when it did, it wasn't nothing. He'd heard people say talk was cheap, but that wasn't true. Talk was magic, it turned the world, it was power when you knew how to fuse it with what mattered and pull your actions taut inside it like arrows.

Talk had made him what he was. Talk was his unique gift and his inheritance: he was born to a nation of talkers, a nation where you stopped by for a minute and stayed for hours, chatting over wine or whiskey or yerba mate. Conversation threads and weaves the world. This was an element some foreign reporters didn't understand; they rushed through their list of questions and didn't know how to deepen into the rhythms of exchange. Some reporters showed up so starry-eyed or bent on their own ends that it was clear from the beginning they would only go so deep, so the ex-president kept them on the surface and sent them on their way. Most of the time, when that happened, the reporters seemed content. This woman, though, already seemed different, he could tell just from her gait as she walked up the path; she seemed to have the listening gift, which would make for a different kind of interview, the thought of which, in fact, gave him a sense of the ground falling beneath his feet—though he didn't show it on the outside, trained revolutionary that he was—and what was it, anyway, this shaking inside, it wasn't fear exactly but something else, the prick of temptation, the possible tapping at shells that might want to creak open after all, because who was he kidding, why pretend, of course he still had places that were shut inside and had not yet been poked and found, buried secrets no interview had touched, of course he had parts of the long story he'd never really told no matter how many thousands of interviews he'd given so far, obviously he did, how else could it be, now come on, would an old guerrilla like him really lay it all bare? Sure, he laid it bare, he told it all, he'd been the most honest president in the world, infamous for saying whatever popped into his mind as long as it was true, but even so, he had layers and then more layers, as did any human being. There were intimate versions of your own story you did not give the world. The deeper ones; the strange ones; the ones you yourself drew life from but did not quite fully understand. And that was the problem with the listening gift: it widened the whole channel, and next thing you knew you were waxing on, you were roaming out, you didn't know what you'd say next or what would crack open. The woman was in front of him now, holding out her hand to shake in that First World way, her face warm, her cameraman just behind her. To his absolute surprise, the ex-president felt the past rise inside him with a roaring fullness, and even though he knew he wouldn't tell it—he'd never told it, would never tell it, knew it couldn't be conveyed in words—he felt it push alive in him, that closed-up secret, that deep-sea story from forty years ago, the one that could answer half their questions in one swoop, the story of the frog.

＋＞＜＋

There was almost no light in that damn hole. He was alone. He'd been locked up for four years so far, and he was dead inside. There was, of course, no end in sight: there was no sentence, as there had been no trial, so that hole or whatever hole they chose for him would be the world as long as the dictatorship held sway. The day he first met the frog, he'd taken a shit in a corner because he couldn't wait for the daily hooded trip down to the toilet and he knew he might get a beating for what he'd done but so what, he thought, another beating, what else is new. What a shitty place, he thought to himself, and he imagined his old comrades laughing at the unoriginal joke, imagined himself laughing though his body couldn't muster the response. He knew that two of his comrades, brothers-in-arms, were also somewhere nearby, or had been when he first arrived; they'd been transported in the back of the same military truck, from the last set of cells to these, all blindfolded but able to whisper just enough to ascertain they were there. But that was only in the truck; once the transport was over, the cargo was stowed in strict isolation. However close or far those comrades were, they were also out of reach. He could not hear them, they could not hear him. A meter, a kilometer, a span of stars—what did it matter when the dampening was complete. Alone. The only light slithered in through four slits in a metal cover over his head which the guards slid aside to lower him into the cell or to pull him up at toilet time. Food came down in a bucket tied to a rope. From the weak crawl of that one slant of broken light, he knew it was day. The dirt was rank, he was sore in so many places that he'd lost track, and he was disconnected from his own body, unable to comprehend it, as if it were a book written in a language you've started to forget.

The world was over.

It turned out that the world could end, and abandon you in it still alive, lost, with nothing left with which to save it.

The movement, his friends, his family, their safety, anyone's safety, a country where it was possible to breathe. All gone. The country as he'd known it was gone. He'd fought for it to become a better place and instead it had collapsed, a country can collapse and turn to rubble. The world was rubble and so was he. For weeks, at least he thought it was weeks, he'd been talking to the ants and scattered spiders who paraded through the hole. His repugnance toward them had disappeared, overshadowed by his repugnance toward himself. What's a harmless line of ants in the face of all the disgusting shit in the corner and his rib cage and his mind? Hello, he'd say to them, what are you doing today, what are you carrying, is it heavy, is it tasty, are you free, where are you going? And you, spider, do you like it on my thigh, fine then, why not, sit right there, what the fuck does it matter anyway and tell me, where were you born, where are you going to die, not on my thigh I'll tell you that much because why would I crush you, haven't we all had enough of that?

But none of them ever answered—not the ants, nor the spiders, nor the dirt or shaft of light—until the day in question, when a voice cut through the grime.

Good day.

He looked around, up at the hole cover, to this side and that.

Good day.

I've finally lost my mind, he thought. A pouring of relief.

Down here.

He looked down. A frog. Not small, not large, a brown-ish green, eyes like pools of liquid black. Unblinking.

You?

Me, yes. What—you can talk to the ants but not to me?

You heard me thinking?

I hear you fine.

But I didn't say anything aloud.

Which is unfair. With the ants you never shut your trap. For the spiders you're like a little old lady, laying out the fancy china and chattering on about the houseplants. But me? For me? You won't even speak?

He sat frozen. He hadn't spoken—had he? Was it possible he'd lost even that, the power to distinguish between thought and speech? Perhaps he'd know more if he consciously used his voice. He cleared his throat. "This isn't happening."

Ha, ha, then tell me, you, if this isn't happening, what is?

The frog didn't open its mouth when it spoke, but its throat moved to the exact rhythm of its words.

"Go away."

Really. You're in this stinking hole alone, and your only visitor, you tell to go away.

"I— Get out of here." He couldn't have explained why he clenched inside, what made him go cold then hot all over, but his mouth was open and he heard screaming and he'd already learned, from the early days, that the screams were always his own. "Go on, scram!"

You're an asshole.

And, with that, the frog hopped off into a corner and disappeared.

➤➤◄◄

For two days, after the frog's first visit, the man waited for it to return. But it didn't come. He decided, in a moment of lucidity—his belly was not exactly full but the closest it had been in days, lined by a layer of thin gruel—that he'd imagined the whole thing. He'd finally lost his grip on reality. Well, good, all the better, and about time too, fuck reality, he thought, I don't want to hold it anymore my fingers hurt too much for that.

Four years of incarceration. No contact with other humans. Deep solitary.

Even the guards who thrust food his way were not allowed to speak to him.

Staying human could be a burden sometimes, in all the kinds of times, the torture and also the loneliness, the heat and also the cold, the hunger and thirst, darkness and a plague of too much light, silence and a plague of loud guards. To go insane seemed a gift, then, a yielding sweetness, a permission to let go and float away, a slipping of your mind's tired hands, he'd finally arrived, could at last loosen his hold on his damn mind, stop fighting to maintain a human shape. But no. No. Guerrilla training rose up in him, shamed him for flirting with the temptation. He did not have permission. Who did he think he was. Madness had its dangers, after all. If he let his mind break entirely, and they tortured him again: then what?

What would he say?

Who might he give away?

What would he be capable of?

They'd all drilled it into each other and into the younger comrades as they joined the struggle: for a revolutionary, insanity was a danger zone, a forbidden luxury, something you couldn't afford, and never did anyone mention the possibility that it might not be a choice, that insanity might maul you whether you accepted it or not. Everything had to be aligned. Everything disciplined, in its place, for the sake of the revolution.

So close it had seemed, the revolution, back then. He'd been able to taste it in the wind, glimpse it in the blur of streetlights shrouded in dark rain, in the pursed lips of comrades whose real names he never learned but with whom he'd risked his life, these men and women, younger than him, so young they were almost kids. All of them catching the scent of revolution in the air, drunk on it or sobered by it depending on the way you looked at things and, in his imprisonment, he'd had a lot of time, too much, to look at things from every possible angle. Every millimeter of thought given its due. The dream had been within their reach, about to happen. Around the corner. And then destroyed. Now his body and his country were destroyed. His body he could stand to lose, but his country, his beloved little country at the bottom of the world— this was the ruin that clawed at his heart. A country can be killed and flayed, like a dog, like a man. This was something he hadn't known before it happened, something he hadn't really imagined, even when the conversations at secret meetings grew dire, even when studying the cases of other fallen nations, even then, he hadn't been able to truly grasp the thought that an entire country—not the people in it, but the *country* itself—could be so fragile. Now it was done. There was no hope. Hope was the skin that had been flayed. Everyone was locked up or had fled for their lives or had shut down in terror, prisoners and exiles and people in hiding, freedom and safety were things of the past, so that, really, when he thought about it, the rigorous training that kept rearing up might not be so relevant after all; it might be that he could afford to lose his mind if he could just ascertain he didn't need it, that it didn't matter, that there was no one left to save.

T he other haven was to die.
   Death and madness, verdant fields just out of
   reach. They blurred into each other. Touch one
and the whole universe might turn green. Closer, closer,
close enough to taste.

—➤—◄—

The frog returned. Where he'd been for the past three days, it was impossible to know. The man knew three days had passed because the morning light through the slats had woken him, dim as it was, shaken him rudely out of sleep each time and forced him to begin a long slow staring at the wall. But now, on this day, when the man who would one day be president saw the creature crouched in the shadows, he thought, with a slight lift to his spirits, it's happened, you've done it now, you've gone insane, after all these hours of wondering yes or no like pulling petals off a daisy—I've lost my mind, haven't lost my mind, I have the right to lose it, no I don't—you just might have an answer. Well then. Welcome company. If I'm going to be unhinged and forced to stay alive, better to at least have someone to talk to.

"You're back."

And you? Are you still an asshole?

Not what he'd hoped for. He felt himself deflate. "That's how it's going to be between us?"

Why not?

Hope swallowed by disgust. "Because."

Ooooooh! Because!

"Leave me alone."

Why should I?

"I'm trying to die."

Well that's stupid.

"What?" He was taken by surprise, couldn't think how to respond. The nerve. If this frog was a figment of his own warped mind, what right did it have to insult him? "Go take a shit somewhere."

I see you've already taken care of that.

"Ha ha, very funny."

It really is stupid.

"Shitting?"

Trying to die.

"No, it's not. You don't get it." Something cracked open inside him, released—what? Not anger. Not exactly. He didn't know what it was. "The world is broken, it's gone, it's all over."

That's what you think.

"How could I think anything else? Have you been out there?"

I've been out there and I've seen the sun.

"Lucky bastard."

Well? Have you been out there?

"You think I was born in this hole?"

And so. When you were out there, did you see the sun?

He was not the frog, the frog was not his mind, how else could his questions prod and startle like this? "I did." His memory swerved to the Before, and he thought of his plants, his flowers, the tender stalks he raised in the back courtyard and then cut to sell at open-air markets, the smiles of old ladies as he gave them compliments along with the wares so they'd feel young again as they gathered the blooms to their chests to take home and arrange in their cluttered living rooms, a reprieve from sadness and nostalgia, comfort in a vase, gifts for the graves, petals to catch the sun, a humble trade but one with which he'd proudly supported himself and his mother, but no, stop, he couldn't bear it, he would not think of his mother, not here and not like this. "Of course I did."

Then you should be better in the knowing.

"Huh?"

You don't know a thing.

Now he *was* angry. "Neither do you."

The frog cocked its head. An unexpected pose. Frogs, then, could cock their heads; he never would have guessed. It was strange how fast this creature could tangle him in thoughts, so fast he forgot who—what—he was talking to. What the hell did it mean? Better in what knowing? So what about the sun?

I'm not the one planning to die in here.

"I'm not—I don't— Oh, shut up."

Fine, the frog said, and the man was surprised to feel a pang of regret as the frog hopped away.

—➤——◂—

W e were thrilled," the reporter said, "when you granted us this interview. We know you have many demands on your time."

The ex-president smiled. "And here you are."

"Yes." She let her gaze rove the room. "Here we are."

They were in the kitchen, where, as he'd guessed, the cameraman had wanted to get footage before settling down outside. The trick, when a camera hovered near, was to act as if it wasn't there. The more natural the better, he knew, and natural was certainly what suited him. In recent years, hundreds of cameras had entered this house, a three-room building that was regular to his eyes, enough for him and his wife, but whose size he'd seen in a new way when he first went to work in the presidential office at the center of the capital. That office—the room itself—was twice the size of his entire house; what was he supposed to do with all that empty space? Over the course of his presidency the space filled with gifts from all over the world, from kings, from rock stars more famous than kings. He'd worked there during the day and returned each evening to the little farmhouse he called home, and still, always, it was more than enough for him. He didn't exactly reject that unofficial title he'd been given, the Poorest President in the World—he knew people used it in admiration or affection—but he did refute it when given the chance. I am not poor, he'd say, because after all, what does it mean to be wealthy? The truly rich are those who want for nothing, who have everything they need, so if you keep your needs simple and are able to fulfill them, you're rich. Meanwhile, the true poor are people with a lot of money who keep running after more. Or doing terrible things for more. Especially them, they're the most impoverished of all, because their spirits are destitute, their spirits are in ruins. And in that case, tell me, who is really the poorest president in the world?

Mate. He'd prepare some yerba mate. A logical thing to do when you're in your kitchen with a moment to spare. He put the water on to boil. "Did you fly in today?" he asked.

"Yes," the reporter said. "It took three flights to get here from Oslo."

Oslo. Hmm. Neither Germany nor Sweden then, but Norway. A small country, he knew, though perhaps not as small as his own. It was a strange thing that had happened to his reputation, its spread around the world; it continued to startle him whenever he caught some glimpse of his popularity abroad. In some ways, he was even more beloved in countries beyond his own. It's the people who watch you lead up close who see your warts and pockmarks, have reason to feel let down by what you couldn't solve. But this was no time to get bogged down by that. The ex-president went about preparing the yerba mate leaves in the gourd, filling it to two-thirds and slanting the leaves to create a hollow on one side, pouring drops of cold water into the hollow so the yerba wouldn't scald, and sliding in the metal bombilla that served as a straw. The most comforting of rituals. He never took it for granted, the freedom to make yerba mate. Not since he'd spent years without it. Without so many things. When the water was ready, the old man poured it into a thermos, poured from the thermos into the gourd, drank first, refilled the gourd, and offered it to the cameraman, who shook his head apologetically, then to the reporter, who took it with a delicacy that bordered on reverence. Was the reverence for the gourd, or for the man handing it over? How on earth did this woman see him? How strange it was, the inability to ever fully see yourself through another person's eyes.

"That metal straw, that's the bombilla—don't stir it around," he warned, "whatever you do."

She froze at this new information, as foreigners usually did when on the brink of transgression. She'd been about to do it. They always wanted to. There seemed to be something human, almost primal, about the impulse to stir.

"It has to stay still, or else the leaves get stuck where they shouldn't and the flow is gone."

"I see," the reporter said. She drank. She took a few sips, then handed back the gourd. "It's very nice," she said politely. He filled the gourd for himself, and felt the bitter liquid warm his throat and wake his mind. He refilled and looked questioningly at the reporter, but on this round she declined. Nevertheless, she'd joined the ronda—the yerba mate circle—and though some did, some didn't, and it was fine either way, everyone should be free to do as they liked with their mouths and every other part of themselves; after all, he'd fought for such freedoms all his life, hadn't he, even so the ex-president felt the gesture as a closing of distance, a drawing of her closer into his world, for the ronda always gently wove people together, as if the gourd traced an invisible webbing from hand to hand.

"Shall we go outside?" she said.

He nodded and put the gourd and thermos on the counter with a slight pang; something to look forward to when the interview was done.

In the garden by the patio, adjacent to the house, the reporter and cameraman arranged the two chairs as they saw fit and then the ex-president and the reporter sat down, facing each other. The cameraman started setting up his tripod. The air was warm, stirred by a delicate breeze. The treetops rustled gently and the grass stood gilded in light. The ex-president took a slow breath, then another, staring out at the riotous leaves, imagining that they received his exhalation as a welcome, ingesting his air, exhaling oxygen, a gift for animal lungs and he was an animal after all and bound to them by the circling air, basic science really but he found it helpful to tune in to it each day. Breathe with the plants. Alive. A simple thing to do, but how often it had caught him, carried him back into his skin after a long day's work. He was happy to be outside, surrounded by so much green. He was also happy to be sitting down, though he wouldn't have admitted it aloud. His joints were crotchety today, it hurt to stand. Old age astounded him, almost every day; he'd spent so much of his youth and middle age convinced he'd never reach it. He resisted the urge to scratch his leg where the bullet wounds were, gnarled skin beneath his trouser leg.

"So this," the reporter said, looking around her slowly, "is your famous garden."

The ex-president raised his eyebrows, didn't hide his pleasure, and really, he thought, why should I? On so many other matters, he took the modest tack, down-played the power he held, waved away words of praise, carried himself with humility, but on this subject, his garden, he allowed himself the luxury of pride.

"And you tend to it yourself?"

"Yes. My wife gets in there too, but it's mostly me. No outside gardeners, that's for sure."

"And you grow vegetables."

"Oh yes—down that way." He gestured to the path, curving past a thick green bush. "We can go later if you like, I can show you."

"That would be wonderful. What do you grow there?"

"Oh, everything. Tomatoes, zucchini, onions, basil, parsley, carrots, cucumbers, lettuce, chard . . ."

"So many things," she said, and her admiration sounded genuine.

He wondered whether the reporter grew any plants, back in Oslo. Whether she knew the pleasures and demands of roots and dirt. She showed no signs of it; her appearance was sleek and tidy, in her black T-shirt and blazer, a professional woman at the cutting edge of the world, but that meant nothing, she could still have a secret or not-so-secret love of gardening that rose to the surface in her private life. Everything was possible in private life. "Yes, of course, we cultivate the things we need, which means things that feed us as well as those that are beautiful."

"Such as flowers."

"Absolutely, such as flowers."

"Their beauty fulfills a need?"

"Don't you believe that?"

She paused, at the edge of answering, then smiled her way back into her role as the bearer of questions. "And the vegetables, do they feed you—that is, you eat them?"

"Yes, of course."

"And your flowers feed you in another way."

"Yes." He settled back into his chair, let his hands rest against each other in his lap. "I've always grown flowers."

"So I've learned, from reading about you. What an interesting trade."

"Is it?"

"From florist to president."

"Most people say, from guerrilla to president. Or from political prisoner to president. They seem to find it more dramatic."

The irony of his remark was not lost on her, and yet she

kept her expression steady and neutral. "Are they more dramatic?"

He felt her looking into him. Tap-tap, what's there. "None of those are more or less dramatic, they're all my life, and all the true parts of a person's life are worth telling."

She smiled, as if encouraging him to go on. But he did not.

The silence gathered between them, a comfortable thing. He remembered what another Norwegian reporter had said to him years ago, just after he was elected president, *People don't always understand that our culture is comfortable with silences, at home in them.* He felt it now, the lack of restlessness, the ability to curl up in a silence as if by a fire, as if silence could be a warm hearth on a cold night, a gentle nesting place for the mind. Had he spent time in the company of Norwegians since then? He was certain he had—so many gatherings at embassies and international summits through the years—but not, perhaps, in such an intimate space, just the three of them, the Norwegians and him. It could seem quiet, a space of three, but you never knew, anything could happen, every word was unscripted until it came, and isn't that it, he thought, isn't that exactly what's so terrible and exhilarating about it all? Ha, look at that, an eighty-something-year-old man contemplating the exhilaration of daily life. He'd have guessed the thrills would all be behind him by now. And yet you can arrive at old age to find the opposite to be true—that intensity could persist at this stage of life, only with a different texture, spurred by the smallest and most ordinary things.

Angelita loped up to the reporter and sniffed around her knees.

"What a sweet little dog."

"She's my favorite," the ex-president said. "Our other dogs all know it, everybody knows it, so there's no need to sugarcoat. She's the one who's got me at her beck and call."

The reporter leaned forward for a closer look. "She lost a leg?"

His chest tightened. "It was an accident, with a tractor." He'd been the one. He'd been behind the tractor's wheel as the dogs played and roiled around him, too close, he hadn't seen—he pushed the memory away. A wrenching accident. The leg was lost but Angelita was saved over the course of long hours that blurred too brightly in his memory, all blood and horror and light and sweat down his back as he raged inside *don't die, don't die*. Angelita did not die. She walked slowly and awkwardly, but her spirits were unblemished, she was the same sweet-tempered dog and, miracle of miracles, harbored not the slightest drop of rancor toward the man who'd driven over her and crushed her bones. She was completely loyal to him, more loyal than any government official had ever been or could ever be, and not only that, she loved him more each day. And how he loved her back. After the accident, his devotion became absolute, a pure and hallowed thing. He rose early to cook her favorite food, sautéed ground beef, a habit he kept throughout the presidency. Angelita rubbed her head against the reporter's leg, satisfied with what she'd smelled, then trotted over to the former president in that buoyant, uneven way only she had.

"She likes you," he told the reporter.

"I like her."

The former president scratched Angelita behind the ears, felt her melt against him. "Your Spanish is very good."

The reporter smiled, now, with unmitigated delight. "Thank you. It's my great passion. I studied Latin American literature at the university."

"Ah! And what's your favorite Latin American book?"

"My goodness, there are so many." She hovered at the border of a thought, torn, he thought, between falling into the question and keeping to her task. "I've loved many from your country. Do you have a favorite book?"

She was a good interviewer, turning the focus back on him so deftly you might not notice it had happened. *Books saved my life,* he thought of saying, but that answer would take them right into the prison years, the later ones, when he was finally granted permission to read and began to rise up from the unnameable place where he'd been. Too deep. Not yet. Better to use the same strategy that she had. "Many," he said.

The reporter beamed at him, then turned to the cameraman. "Are we ready?"

"Already rolling."

Of course. That age-old trick. Get them talking before they know the recording has started. Not that he was caught off guard; he knew exactly how it was done. What startled him was how far he'd already opened when they supposedly hadn't even begun.

"Let's see," she said. "Thank you so much again, Mr. President, for receiving us."

He nodded, waited. He didn't like being referred to as Mr. President, had never liked it, had harangued all his aides until they finally relented and used his first name, but he'd learned long ago that it took much longer than one interview to break the habit, plus it perturbed some foreigners to wade away from formalities, so what the hell. He'd let it go.

"You have many admirers in Norway."

"That's very kind."

"It's quite true. You're a beacon of hope, giving the world a different view of leadership, showing us that it's possible for a president to truly serve the people."

He raised his eyebrows.

"Don't you believe that to be true?"

Somewhere out of sight, that stubborn thrush had struck up another song. "Well, let's see, how shall I put it? Many things are true."

She leaned forward, gracefully, eyes wide open. "Like what, Mr. President?"

In the cell, bleak days, bleak hours, the keening of the ants wouldn't let him rest. Every time he fell asleep, they'd screech together, first low then rising till his head rang awake. Things had happened in the torture chamber, more than he'd understood, more than he wanted to understand, but also more than surely was believed out there wherever people dared breathe words about it: they hadn't just used La Máquina on his body, wasn't just prods and hoods and water, they'd also implanted something in his brain—he was sure of it, on the bleakest days he was absolutely sure of it—some chip, some radio receptor, some terrible technology imported from, where else, the USA, naturally it would have been made in the USA, given that this country's torturers had been trained by interlopers from that place and now because of that chip receptor he couldn't control his own mind, it hummed in his skull and roared things he didn't want to hear, frequencies, screams, scrambled songs, torn voices, the keening of ants. Turn it off. He had to learn the secret way to turn it off. What mental feat could overcome such an insidious enemy? How do you win when the enemy is implanted in your mind? What superhuman mental strength does it require to lift your thoughts to the right frequency for survival, how to find that strength, where to source it, what's the way? It was a deeply inner battle and he had little left to give. Sometimes, he didn't even want to try. Sometimes he longed only for the stupor of forgetting, a falling as if into sleep, only into a state more numb than sleep, more permanent, a vanishing from which he'd never have to wake.

And yet.

Every time temptation slunk toward him, he found himself rattled by *and yet*.

Stupor was exactly what they wanted from him.

Some other part of his mind, a chip-free part, remembered this and hauled it up to the surface to be heard. Stupor made for an easy prisoner. For a pliant citizen. Fascists love stupor. They insist on stupor. Shut up. Shut down. Become a passive mind. They wanted this from everyone, not just prisoners but also the rest of the people, the ones beyond the prison who pretend they are still free. The ones out on the streets, in their homes, under dictatorship, with that word *under* as if governments could hover as thick dark clouds, brooding, shrouding, everywhere. A fog you can't see through. The people sleepwalking through it, in a haze of distraction and fear. He imagined them, the people on the outside, in the city, in towns, out on rural lands. He pictured what their lives were like now. People he'd loved and fought for. People whom he'd failed. We tried to make a new country for you, he thought. Tried to give you a revolution. Tried to give the country what it needed, what we thought it needed, what we thought you wanted, and it was the opposite of this. I'm sorry. More sorry than you know. Do you hate us? Blame us? Weep for us? Think of us at all?

Come on, wake up.

The frog. A voice so clear it sliced through thought. The sound of it in his ears and rib cage flooded him with relief.

"It's you." He tried to sit up to better see the creature in the dim light. Body stiff and awkward. And no wonder, he thought, I'm past forty after all, too old for this sort of thing, ha, maybe I should tell the guards this whole situation isn't age appropriate, that'll show them. "I wasn't sleeping."

Liar.

"Really, I wasn't."

Your eyes were closed.

"And why not? There wasn't anything to see."

So you were going to droop all day.

With a jolt, he realized the ants had gone quiet. Why? How had the frog's appearance led to relief from the screaming of ants? Had they fled out of fear of being eaten or trampled? Or did the voice of one somehow cancel out the voices of the other? Frog versus ants, the great war for a dirt hole—or for the mind of a man trapped in a hole. Ha. Now, there was a story for Homer's ballads. His mind flashed to it: Homer on an ancient stage or in the corner of a pub or brothel or wherever he first sang his songs, drowning in boos and insults because what a pathetic story, ants and a man in a hole. The image brought fleeting relief, a flicker of comfort, before it disappeared. "Maybe."

Tsk.

"Well? So? What the hell else am I supposed to do?"

Get ready.

"For what?"

The rest of your life.

Laughter rose, rancid, up his throat. "There is no rest of my life. I'm going to spend it here or in hole after hole after hole."

Not true.

"And how would you know?"

The mysteries are a layer and a layer.

"Mysteries?" It was nonsense, of course, but something about the frog's words, the way they hung together, was unnerving. "What, you're a priest now? Because I don't need any of your frog-sermons."

Yes you do.

Something clutched at his heart. He fought to ignore it. "I hate priests. I hate church. I'm sure I'd also hate frog-church."

Oh, you'd love frog-church.

"And how the fuck would you know?"

I know. The frog took a few breaths that inflated its throat, then flattened it. *I know things.*

"Hmmf. Sure you do."

Like that you've barely started.

"Started what?"

Life.

"Ha! Now who's the idiot? My life is over. Over! I'm never getting out of this hole and all the holes after this hole, there's nothing left ahead but a long endless string of them, and if I ever do get out I'll be a wreck— I mean look at me, just look at me—I'm starved, bruised, broken." He hadn't seen himself in a mirror for years, wouldn't want to. Wouldn't dare. "I'd be useless to the world."

Meanwhile the dirt.

"Dirt?"

Yes. Haven't you seen it? All around you, look.

"Yes, why yes, I'm in a rank hole with a dirt floor, I can see dirt, thanks so much for pointing that out."

You haven't even started looking. You can't see it. You're so blind you cannot even see the dirt.

"Now you've really gone off the deep end."

Everything real is in the deep end.

He opened his mouth, couldn't speak, sat gaping. Tried and failed to muster a response. He made a sound that didn't coalesce into a word.

The frog cocked its head slightly, stared for a beat or two, then hopped into a dark corner and vanished, leaving the future president with new thoughts churning through his mind.

———>->—<-<———

This time, the frog came back the very next day. The ants were not yet screaming, the hole was quiet except for the occasional footsteps of guards above his head. The wall he was staring at had long ago become familiar. It was made of mud, impossibly thick. He searched for patterns in the mud, anything at all, but as always he found only chaos punctured by scattered mauling mouths.

Hello.

"Ah! You're back."

Why not.

"Sure, why not." Warmth rose up in him, the kind of warmth one might feel at an unexpected knock at the door, back when knocking didn't yet mean danger, could only mean the arrival of a friend, come in, have a seat, have a yerba mate, the gourd is still fresh, how the hell are you, tell me everything. A normal feeling in vanished days. Now it hurt to recall it. "You should come back every day."

The frog made a sound that was not a word.

"Listen," he said, thinking fast, eager to keep his visitor from leaving at any cost. "Tell me this. Where are you from?"

Around.

"Around here? So are there swamps nearby? Ponds?"

Around.

"That doesn't tell me much."

Tell, tell, tell.

"Wha——? Look, any clues will help. I don't even know what part of the country we're in. They put a blindfold over my eyes and dragged me into a truck and they drove and drove. Are we in the east? The north?"

Everything is north of something else.

For fuck's sake, the man thought, but held back from saying. This was not a human friend. You never knew, with this guy—if you could call a frog a guy—how weird an answer would be. Still: annoying as it was, the frog had a point. What would the relativities of maps mean to this animal's life? Land would be land, with no planetary up or down—but no, focus, don't get caught up trying to enter frog-mind. Keep to the thread. Any thread. Try another approach. And then an idea bloomed open inside

him. "How did you get in here? How do you get out?
Are there pipes, cracks—tell me everything. Maybe, if I
learn enough about this place, there might even be a way
to escape."

For you?

"What's that sound? Are you . . . laughing?"

Sorry—but come on.

"You've got a terrible laugh. Like you're farting, or
fucking—or both at once."

I can't stop. The thought of you—in those pipes—

"It's not so strange, you know. I've done it before."
Pride welled up in him and he didn't try to hold it back; he
had no reason to, it had been so long since he'd felt proud
of anything and here he was, recalling what had been—
and what he truly thought would forever remain—the
greatest accomplishment of his life. "It wasn't a dungeon
like this, but it was a full prison, high security, the works."

You escaped?

"One hundred and six of us. It was insane!" He felt a
pinch at the sound of that last word, but even that didn't
steal his pleasure at the memory.

Tell me the story, tell it, I'm hungry.

"Eh? What does hunger have to do with it?"

I will eat it, your story.

"How the hell do you eat a story? What are you, some

kind of story predator? You think my memories are like your nasty flies?"

Let's go.

"No . . ."

Tell. Me.

"This is even creepier than your laugh."

You want to tell me.

"Damn you. I do."

→>-<←

T he man began to tell: It happened in the days
        before dictatorship, when the country still called
        itself a democracy—though things had already
gone bad, it doesn't take a military takeover for a government to menace its own people, or to control them,
harm them, work against them instead of for them, the
possibility is always there, has always been there in the
structure of government itself, at least here, in América,
not that you'd even know what América is or that there's
any other kind of land beyond it, I'm guessing that to you
land is land, period, but on the other hand what do I know.
Anyway. As I was saying, things had already gone bad.
Newspapers were censored, leaders lied through their
teeth, detainees were tortured, cops shot at protesters like
it was nothing, like they enjoyed it, that had all been going
on for a good while. Thinking of it now it seems an eter-
nity ago, an endless maw of time ago and isn't it strange
how such a wide gap can be leapt over by memory as if it

were nothing, poof, you're back in another time, another life. Back in that other prison at the center of the city. I'd been there for many months already and the government had been making a clean sweep of it, there were over a hundred guerrillas in prison, including many of the core leaders of the movement, like me. The old guard. The masterminds. Men I'd known for years, from labor union days, the organizing-for-a-leftist-rebel-senator days, the high dreaming how-shall-we-change-the-world days. My friends. You have to understand, what we wanted was a better world. I don't know that anyone will believe that from us anymore—or that we'll ever get a chance to tell our story our own way; history belongs to the victors, especially when they're despots; most of those old guard friends are in the same situation I'm in right now, in holes more or less like this one I suppose, no reason to believe we'll ever get out. You're probably the last one to hear this story from my lips, lucky you. Ha. Eh. Where was I. So, back at that prison in the capital, there were all kinds of us from the movement, not just old-timers. There were new recruits, too, young students and workers who'd been inspired to join the struggle for liberation, who'd thrown their whole selves into the dangerous life of revolution. They were so fresh-faced, eager, I felt responsible for them, they all had dreams, they all had mothers, they'd made their choices just as I had but they couldn't possibly see how young they were, not the way I could, at thirty-something years old with police bullet wounds scarring my body and years of living underground before I was caught. I wasn't sure these young men—and the young women too, though they weren't at this prison with us—could see how much they were giving up to join the movement, not the way I could. But that didn't mean they weren't smart or committed: they were both of those things, radiant kids, bringing all their vitality to the movement and no torture or barred doors or harsh guard was going to stop them. They believed the revolution was coming, believed in what their strength could do when merged with the strength of the people. There was this one kid, Alfonso was his name, he'd follow me around the prison yard every chance he got, asking me questions about the inception and inner workings of our organization, many of which I couldn't answer, some of which I answered with jokes to keep his spirits up. He was nineteen, a medical student with perfect grades, awkward and lanky, still a virgin, he didn't come right out and say so but I got the drift. Alfonso, I started telling him, when you get out of here you're going to find a girlfriend. Oh I don't know, Alfonso would answer, the revolution is enough for me. What do you mean, enough! I'd say, but

Alfonso would just laugh and flick his bright eyes away from me, then back. It's only now, years later, as I'm telling this story, sitting here in this hole, that something else occurs to me, that there might have been some other reason Alfonso didn't want to find a girlfriend, that what he wanted wasn't a girl at all, that his passion for the revolution was tied somehow to another passion he couldn't speak. That the hunger in his eyes when he looked at me was for knowledge of the movement, sure, for revolutionary strength, but also—ah, damn. Could it be that? Is it possible it even crossed my mind back then but flitted right past because I didn't want to think about it? Didn't want to see it in his eyes as he looked at me, what he was trying but failing to hide. The thing we always talked about as the worst a man could be. The worst insult. Ugh, no. You know what, forget it. Forget I said any of that. That Alfonso, he was a sweet kid, and I hope he fled the country before it was too late and that now he's free.

So, in any case, most of the founders of the movement were together behind bars. And a few months in, we learned that the head warden was willing to let us meet in an open room if we slipped him enough pesos. Those were the days! When a prisoner could meet with his friends! Not only that, they even let us brew yerba mate for the occasion, to pass around the circle as we talked, such freedom. Stabs me to think about it now. I never imagined I'd spend years of my life without tasting yerba mate, to be frank, I don't know how I'm still alive. Anyway. Those guards: you know what, I'm convinced some of them secretly supported our cause, they did what they had to do to feed their families but deep down I believe they wanted us to win, they knew our dreamed-of future would be better for them and for their kids than the future being made by the jerks in charge, but of course they couldn't say any of that outright, just show it in tiny haphazard acts of goodwill. Be that as it may. We were able to communicate. We'd tried to negotiate for our freedom with the government, in exchange for hostages we'd taken—we'd aimed high, let me tell you, we had quite a collection, we'd kidnapped from the upper ranks: a corrupt judge, the British ambassador, a torture trainer from the CIA (well, that last one was dead by this time but I can't say I shed a tear about it, you can't expect that kind of grief from me, not with the hundreds of my fellow citizens he'd mangled, practicing on beggars, prostitutes, people he thought no one would miss, right in the basement of his mansion he did it, that big country in the North thought it could send a man like that to our poor little country to break its poor little people and we'd just lie down and take it, but no, friend, we did not), and in any case we treated all our hostages as kindly as we could in our People's Prison as we called it—but the government said no, we won't negotiate with terrorists. Instead they swept up more of us and our ranks in the prison swelled. One of the men who showed up was an engineer. We brought him into our meetings to help us dream up the escape. It seemed a crazy dream but we knew that a few decades earlier a group of anarchists had managed to tunnel out of this very place. So where were the tunnels? We had no idea. We brewed another round of yerba mate. Could we find those tunnels, build on them, re-create them, finish what the anarchists had started? The quest began.

We searched for the old tunnels and found them, half-collapsed, as ruined and as precious as an ancient temple. We got to digging. We dug every night, didn't sleep. A cluster of our people on the outside dug too, under a house across the street. It was a masterpiece, that underground tunnel, I'm telling you, dug with exquisite precision, a song of negative space, like a sculpture turned inside out. Each night after digging we covered the hole in the wall of our third-floor cell and hid the dirt we'd taken out in little bags we stashed wherever we could, under beds, in the yard, in cracks we found in the walls of the industrial kitchen where many of us worked.

And then, just a few days before the planned escape, Alfonso's lawyer came to visit, unexpected. Good news, Alfonsito, he said: they're going to set you free. It's such a small thing they got you for, possessing contraband leaflets, pieces of paper bearing the word *revolution*, why should you wither in prison for that, in the old days it wasn't even against the law because free expression used to be protected and yes, I know, these aren't the old days, but still, I told them there was no proof of how you'd gotten the leaflets or what you planned to do with them, and I did it, I got your sentence shortened, you leave on Friday. And the kid, he blanched, because the escape was set for Saturday. For weeks now he'd been picturing himself burrowing through that tunnel with the rest of us and it was like he'd been preparing for some sort of descent into the mysteries or I don't know what, but in any case he'd gotten attached, so he tells the lawyer, No thanks, ask them to hold off. What? the lawyer said, eyes bulging from his head. Hold off on what? On getting me out of here, Alfonso says, then follows up with some rambling excuse about how the government's crackdown isn't over yet and maybe he's safer behind bars, at least for now. The lawyer huffs off—he'd come in so proud of his accomplishment on getting his client released and here goes his client, rebuffing the gift—and next thing you know the word's traveled through the city's lawyer grapevine that the political prisoners have some reason they want to stay behind bars.

Alfonso came up to me in the yard, beaming. I tore him a new one. You can't do that! I hissed. We can't have the law sniffing around here, getting suspicious! Alfonso looked a bit crushed, so I softened my stance. Look, I said, we've all got to be extremely careful, all right? There's over a hundred men whose freedom is on the line. Nothing we do can ever happen only because we want it. I'm talking guerrilla basics here. The values of revolution. We don't do things only for ourselves, but for the greater whole, eh? Alfonso nodded heartily. That's how I want to be, he said. And then, more bashfully, am I off the list? I took a good look at him, the sunlight in his scraggly hair. No, I said, you're not off the list. This movement is nothing without people like you.

The next night, at 10:00 sharp, we opened the hole and started to descend. The men slipped down and through. One after the other. From the third floor, the second floor, the first. When we reached the bottom of the tunnel, where it turned horizontal, I felt my lungs collapse into themselves, there was no air down there, with two men in front of me and more than one hundred behind, but there was nothing to do but go forward, slinking on our stomachs like primordial creatures of the kind we'd read about in science textbooks, you know, those ancient ancestors who first crawled up onto land, like crocodile fish with hands on their fins, what do I know, you're probably descended from them too, it might not seem too strange for you, the parallel, but for me it was a real leap of the mind. I'd never slithered like that before. I pictured myself as one of those creatures. I pictured myself as a worm, like the ones I'd always found in the garden where I grew vegetables to feed my family and flowers to pay the bills, worms I hated to kill, as a boy it made me cry when my spade accidentally cut one in two. Now I was a worm, in the dark, no need to see. Did you know that earthworms have no eyes? I closed my eyes. I breathed the dirt. I let the dirt become a new kind of air, an old kind of air, a thing my lungs could love. Creature of dirt, I thought as we inched forward, creature of dirt, the only way I could survive this was by letting myself become a creature of dirt, until it seemed our hundred and six bodies had merged into a single long extended whole, a giant worm probing the earth, kneading it, reshaping it from the inside. Creature of dirt on its way to getting free. Forward, forward, forever—and then finally up, up, voices, light. We burst through the floor into the home of an old woman, a butcher, whose shop was on the first floor, and it was into the back room that we sprang, a space full of red meat hanging from hooks, raw bodies everywhere; the old woman had been startled at first that her house was commandeered by subversives a few hours earlier as part of the great escape, but by the time we arrived she'd made coffee for everyone, for these young revolutionaries with their guns and plans and friends bursting through the floorboards, filthy and exploding with life.

That's a good story.

"It's all true."

More.

"What!" He felt stung by the request, so soon after the telling was done. Didn't a good telling merit a pause, a breather, a space in which to let it hum? The time in which a normal audience would applaud, and you could bask in the triumph of it, bathe in the clapping sound or, if he'd been talking to a circle of comrades, bathe in the laughing sound, the throaty *yes* of their enjoyment. It flashed through him, the memory of such times. Hollowed him out. To make demands so soon after the end seemed almost obscene. "After all that!"

More.

"I can't."

Why not?

"I'm tired."

Fuck you.

"Now, wait a minute—"

No, fuck you. It's wrong. After all the talking you did for the rest of them?

"Rest of who?"

The ants, the spiders.

"Oh come on, not that again. Although, wait a second, while we're on the subject, you really heard that?"

Of course I did.

"I didn't see you then. Were you hiding? Eavesdropping? Where were you?"

Doesn't matter. What matters is—

"In the pipes? Come on, you've got to tell me about the pipes—"

Shut up for a second. You told them stories—

"I didn't. I just rambled, talked, I don't even know what I was saying and a rant is not a story, not even close. I just told you the best story I had. When's the last time some sorry guy in a hole told you a story like that? A true one, no less? And you're going to compare it to my rambling with the spiders?"

You let them all get nice and fat on your voice and now, with me, you're threatening to shut your trap.

"Well. Maybe that's because you don't shut yours."

Hunh!

"Just saying." Though he was bluffing and it made him

nervous; in truth—he couldn't deny it—he didn't want to lose the frog's company or voice.

It's wrong, I tell you. I want stories. Want to eat your stories.

"That makes no sense."

I have no need of sense.

"It's also creepy. Like you're some sort of froggy Dracula. Wanting to suck my voice up like it's blood."

So what. Let me taste.

"What? This can't be happening, it must be another nightmare."

Pinch yourself.

"Ouch! You're right, fucking hell, I can't wake up."

So then you stay in this awake and here you give me more.

"You're a greedy one, you know that?"

The frog tilted its head and stared without blinking; could frogs blink? Had he ever seen this one do it? *That is not the why.*

"Huh?"

There is another why. Give me taste.

"Why should I?"

Because you need to.

"No I don't."

You do, your life depends on it.

"What the hell? Why?"

You'll see.

→>◂‹-

He circled around several beginnings of stories, like a vulture circling bones. There was this, there was that, there was a time. His confidence was shaken now, and he'd started to want the frog's approval, though he didn't want to admit it and couldn't have said why. With each false start, the frog stayed impassive, didn't even croak. No sign. So the man picked the thread that shone the most, and let it lead him down the labyrinth.

Once there was a time, he said, when two soldiers were beating a man, and the man was me, though it wasn't here in this cell but in another, about three different cells ago, and on that day or night—I had no way to know the time—my mind reached out for something, anything, a thought to carry me over the river of pain. The people. That's what came to me. I'd given everything for the people, sworn my life to their freedom, and so perhaps my love for the people could carry me toward a shore.

That's the only thing my mind could find to cling onto. And so, curled up on the ground, trying to shield my skull because I knew well that a broken rib was one thing and a broken skull another, I expanded my mind out to every single one of them, the people, expanded my consciousness like a sphere, like one of those shields of power you see beaming from heroes in comic books, and I let it enfold the people of my country, all of them, the sad ones, the dead-inside ones, the disappointed-in-the-revolution ones and the made-mousy-by-fear-of-the-regime ones, the ones at the market and the ones at the office, at school or in bed, determined or downtrodden, chin high or head hung low, groomed or scruffy as so many of my countrymen can be, male or female, young or old, the ones with plenty of food in the house and the ones picking at that last crust of bread or breaking it into ever smaller pieces for the children, the ones surely afraid these days and that had to be most everyone, the ones who see how bleak the future looks with nobody reliable at the wheel, the ones who still rise from bed in the morning and braid hair and boil water and burn the toast despite the bleakness of the future, the ones distracting themselves with soccer or whiskey or sex or the pouring of yerba mate with trembling hands, I bathed my mind in the people and I still love you, I said to them with my inner voice as I heard as if from a distance my outer voice moan from a blow, I am still here, and as long as you're still breathing I'll breathe too. I reached out toward the people the way others reach for God. A god called Us. That's the best way I can find to express what I did; I reeled my mind outward to embrace the great Us.

This lasted for a few soft moments but then it fell apart and let me tell you why, though I hate to say it: the people are beautiful but they're also chaos.

Somewhere in the city, shuffled in with everybody else, live the guards, torturers, generals who gave all the unthinkable orders, wives who smile tightly over tea and intricate pastries bought with money earned by acts of torture, and my imagination insisted on including them too, for all that I wanted only to embrace the Us that I could bear. Here, right here over me were two soldiers and how I wished I could pretend they were not part of the People. My training had taught me not to see them as the People, but as the opposite, enemies of the People, or at least victims of enemies of the People who'd brainwashed them into what they'd become, and of course that's what they were, enemies or the puppets of enemies, what else, here they were after all doing their day's work, but their hands were too real, they were flesh, they were too human, they disturbed my roaming, punctured it, tore holes in the wide cloth of my love. And where did it stop? If a revolutionary's work is to free the people, *all* the people, then what about the supposed enemies, the soldiers and the sergeants and the children who welcomed them home after a long day of treating prisoners like human filth—of course they'd welcome them, the children would, they'd fling their arms wide the way children do, what else did they know and who could blame them—I did not blame them—and what about the soldiers, they weren't children but they weren't old either, some of them couldn't yet grow a proper mustache, nor had they been raised in the mansions of the rich, their hands, it hurt, everything hurt, the stretching open of my love hurt terribly now, it stabbed at me, as if I were a flag that had unfurled too far and gotten shredded by a violent wind, it was too much, I reeled my mind back in and came back at blinding speed to the body beaten on the ground.

༺ ⬩➤⬩⬩ ༻

T*hat one's not so good.*

 "Oh no?"

 It doesn't go anywhere.

"Huh, I'm so sorry to disappoint you. I was just trying to give you what you asked for."

We're never going to find it at this rate.

"Find? Find what?"

It's not for me to tell, not of my telling.

"Some story feast you can really suck on? Damn, you're strange."

No. Not that. I taste along the way, but the other part is for you.

"I have no clue what you're talking about with this other part. What is it?"

I have said. It is a for-you.

"Eh—well then." Curiosity prickled him, he couldn't help it. The urge to mock the frog's odd way of speaking rose and fell. "Something we, eh, have to find?"

Yes.

"Number one, that makes no sense—"

You don't need sense.

"That's where you're wrong. Yes I do. Everybody does."

Sense is not the need.

"Huh? I don't— Where was I? Second of all. What was it—right, second of all, how will we ever find anything if you don't explain it better? Why don't you just tell me what we're looking for?"

Rain.

"Huh?" The answer was rain, he thought wildly, rain was the answer, but then what had the question been, his head hurt and—

Outside it's going to rain.

"Oh." Not the answer, then. He wasn't sure whether he felt disappointed or relieved. "I sure wish it would rain in here, I'm fucking thirsty."

The frog's eyes seemed to glow in the dim light.

"How do you do that?"

Do what?

"Make your eyes glow?"

How does the sun shine, how does the rain pour.

"That makes no sense."

Who cares?

"Not you, that's for sure, you've made that pretty clear."

Thank you! Thanks to you!

"Calm down! Thing is, we're going in circles now. I still don't know how we'll have a conversation without sense."

We're having one.

"Damn it, I suppose you're right."

Justice.

"What about it?"

Justice next.

"Ha! Justice, never." Acrid in his mouth. "There's no such thing."

Tell me a justice story.

The man opened his mouth to protest, to insist he would not be told what to do, but the lie caught in his throat; of course he could be told what to do. He was a guerrilla, after all; no matter how much he'd moved up the ladder of power, he'd never stopped following commands. Without commands there was no order. Without order there was no strength, without strength you did not win. That's what they had been told and what he'd taught the new recruits, for better or for worse, and he didn't want to think about which it had been for, better or worse. And look at you now, he thought bitterly to himself, some revolutionary, taking commands from a frog. And yet they didn't seem so foreign, not so different, after all, from other kinds of commands; granted, this wasn't like receiving directives from higher movement ranks, but it did feel like listening to the dirt when planting flowers, letting it tell you how much water, where to sink roots. So. A justice story. What was that anyway. The future president set off on a search through the rubble of his mind.

→►─◄←

They'd been talking for a while now, the reporter and the ex-president, with the cameraman hovering in the background, a silent witness. They'd discussed a range of topics, from the far past to the recent, the personal and the presidential, layers that, to him, had their own distinct shapes yet also overlapped and never became entirely separate, like ocean waves. How could anyone stop being their inner self, just because they happened to be head of state? You brought who you were with you. Gaining power didn't change what you were, though it could magnify certain parts of you. So far he'd managed to avoid any new disclosures, though his story with the frog still prickled at the edges of thought. The thrush had gone quiet again. In the distance, cars occasionally rumbled by.

Now she rounded toward the subject of laws he'd passed, while president, the progressive legislation with which he'd transformed the face of—

"Not me," he said, "but we."

"Sorry?"

"Laws are passed by a *we*." He closed his eyes for just an instant, saw green, leaf green, then opened them. "That's very important. Congress was part of it, and so were the people who voted us in and who came to us with proposals and demands for what they wanted to see. Laws are like revolutions: it's never one person who brings them into being."

"Unless that person is an authoritarian," the reporter said.

The ex-president spread his hands open. "People may accuse me of many things, but I don't see how they can accuse me of that."

"Indeed." She nodded. "To be frank, I've never heard new laws compared to revolutions."

"Ah."

She waited a few beats and, when he didn't elaborate any further, pressed on. "Your wife is in Congress—and she was also in Congress during the years in which you"—now she used the plural form of *you*—"passed these transformative laws."

"Indeed. And she's a force of nature." He remembered how it was between them soon after he won the election, how they sat for hours one morning drinking yerba mate at the kitchen table, at the same kitchen table from which they'd run all their campaigns and made decisions both national and intimate, large and small. What have we gotten ourselves into? he'd said, taking the mate gourd from her so he could serve the next round. *A presidency,* she'd said. My God, he'd replied, pouring water into the gourd, drinking, until the last of the liquid gurgled in the leaves, when you say it I can't believe my ears, it's really happening, who would ever have guessed. *Can you imagine,* she said, *the turns our lives have taken, what a journey, what a tale.* Straight out of García Márquez, he agreed, handing her a full gourd. As she took it, she said, *Do you know what's really funny? Guess who'll be swearing you in?* He hadn't thought that far ahead, submerged as he'd been in the campaign. So he said, I give up, who? *Me! Not as your wife, but as Senate Majority Leader!* They stared at each other then. You! he said. *Me,* she said. *And. You.* And then they laughed until their sides hurt and tears caught in the wrinkles around their eyes. "She's always been a force."

"Doesn't the president have a particular role, though, in leading the charge for political change?"

"What a lot of people don't understand is that power is not singular. It doesn't come from one person or belong to one person. It belongs to the hive. A leader channels that power, but it doesn't belong to him, and there's no power without the hive."

"This is assuming a democracy."

"This is anywhere."

"You say this"—her voice went gentle, cautious—"having lived through a dictatorship."

"Sure."

"Authoritarians don't see it that way."

"No."

"Do they destroy the hive?"

"They try to. But no. They might wipe out the swarm but they can't destroy the hive."

"Is that what's coming now in the U.S.? Authoritarianism?"

"Ah . . ." He raised his eyebrows. Here it was. The subject of the North, the disaster there and what it might unleash, which they hadn't yet touched but which he'd felt lurking at the edges of the garden, skulking, biding its time. Deep breath. Part of him wished he could talk instead about the way the sun had started gilding the tree branches, but then he chided himself, come on, old man, let's go.

But before he could speak, the reporter broke in.

"You know what," she said, looking slightly disoriented, as if startled by her own question. "Let's not broach that yet."

She looked away, toward the path that led down to the vegetable garden. He sensed fear beneath her words, and something else too, a charge he couldn't quite define. He waited.

"We'll have to at some point—that is, I'll want to— but that's not where we were, let's go back to discussing more hopeful things."

"Why not," said the ex-president, thinking of but not mentioning the sun in the trees.

"The legislation that passed, here in this country, during your presidency. It seems to me that it changed the shape, not only of civil rights, but of the culture. And some of it did so beyond your borders, these laws made international waves, served as examples. The legalization of marijuana and of gay marriage and first-trimester abortions. The affirmative action law for Black citizens. All very hopeful."

"Are they?" he said.

"Why wouldn't they be?"

He pictured telling her about the context around each law, the complicated territory, the clamor from activists insisting that the push must continue, that these laws weren't enough, the women's groups with their *what about the second trimester? What about teens who can't get parental consent? And what about other issues, like domestic violence?* and the racial justice groups with their reams of grim statistics about ongoing inequality, they'd only scratched the surface, what about the displacement of Black people during the dictatorship, how would those neighborhoods be restored, what about racial disparities in education, economic disparities that refused to budge, racism ran centuries deep here as it did throughout the Americas, it was systemic, one law wouldn't cut it, there was so much work to be done. And it was true. A great deal of work remained to be done. The affirmative action law, and the other laws, were just single stops along the road. They were not finished with the creation of a just country, far from it, they'd only just started. It would be the work of generations, not one administration but many, each building on the work of the last one if they were lucky enough to avoid a full pendulum shift to the right. Meanwhile, he had plenty of dissatisfied constituents who believed progress had been too slow on this or that front, and who might not hold the laws the reporter had mentioned in the same optimistic light. Within the country, their impact was contested. And yet, it seemed better, today at least, for now at least, to allow the accomplishments to glow for other countries, to shine toward them; look, something has been done, little by little and stitch by stitch we can reweave the world. "Hope is for something to happen in the future, these laws are here."

"Well, they give hope to us in the rest of the world."

"That's good." He remembered the day he signed each law, the quality of light in the Presidential Palace as he sat at his desk surrounded by senators. Before his presidency, he'd always thought of the signing of laws as a formality, nothing more, but once he started taking part in the experience he'd come to see something deeper in it, something archetypal, a kind of totemic moment. A circle of bureaucrats around you, like a circle of druids. The lure of ritual. Legal decree as two-dimensional witches' brew. Humans need rituals. He was an atheist, but that didn't mean he couldn't see their power. Ritual spoke to the deeper reaches of the human mind. Still, he liked to spike those hallowed moments with touches of the profane, as if to say, look, the profane and the hallowed, they belong together, they're made to intermix. The day he signed the gay marriage law, he took a pen from his aide's hand—an old Bic whose end had been chewed by someone or other's restless teeth, because any pen would do to make a law, even the simplest ink can do it, it was really quite amazing, sign your name and the law comes alive, the air

shifts somehow across the land—and as he turned toward
the page that would bring the law into being he thought
of young Alfonso, the revolutionary, the one with whom
he'd done time at the prison in the city, Alfonso whose
ultimate whereabouts he'd never learned. Perhaps he'd
managed to flee the country and avoid years of prison;
perhaps he'd been locked up and gotten out when democracy returned. Perhaps he'd even found a way to live the
life he was supposed to live, to follow the spark that all
those years ago he'd fought to hide, if, in fact, the president was right about what he thought he'd seen decades
ago. A spark that everybody knew to be disgusting. See-
ing it in Alfonso had been the first time it had occurred
to him to think of it any other way. Even now, he swung
between perspectives: looking down on people like that
was discrimination, no, it was common sense, facts of
nature, no, it had to be seen as discrimination after all.
At the end of the day, he still couldn't understand exactly
what made a man want a man or a woman want a woman,
but he also knew he didn't have to understand these things
to change the law, for nobody was forcing him to marry
a man, now, were they? He agreed on that much with the
gay activists who'd come to him and Congress demand-
ing change. They'd shown up, young and old, male and
female, and even a few who'd transmuted from one to

the other and claimed the word *transgender,* all of them right there in the open, some flagrant, others looking like any nice auntie or bespectacled student or kiosk vendor and you never would have known, only there they were, united, insistent, filling his office, passing the yerba mate among them as they talked. This is about equal rights, they'd said. And who could argue with equal rights? The revolution—such as it was, whatever that word meant these days—had to be for everyone, period. He didn't have to understand or even like every detail of other people's lives to know they deserved to be free. More than that: they had a right to be free. That may have been a flaw of their revolution in the old days, that it left out the transformation of culture, where so much caging and liberation took place. And if—so many ifs—if Alfonso was still alive; if he was here in the country rather than having made a home in exile; if he did indeed have that spark inside him and if he'd found some way to recognize that spark, then this law might mean something to him. It was a lovely morning, the ripe end of summer, and a lush beam of sunlight fell over the written version of the law; it warmed his skin as he bent forward to add his signature to the embossed page.

"It certainly is good," the reporter said, calling the ex-president back into the moment. "We've always needed it, but we especially need it right now. Certainly the television-viewing public in Norway wants to hear about it. Some of the actions have been executive, as when you told the United States you'd take in prisoners from Guantánamo."

"Right. Well. They'd been held without trial all those years and needed a refuge, a place to go. It's up to each nation to ask itself what it can do to foster peace." Another circumstance that had become more complicated than he'd anticipated, but if she didn't ask, he wouldn't wade in, no reason to disturb her sunny impressions of what he'd tried to do, especially since such attempts were usually interpreted by foreign journalists as false modesty. He'd meant well. That much was straight-up true. He'd done his best to help clean up another country's mess, and not just any other country, but the one that had backed the coup in his own nation and trained the very torturers who'd tortured him, but that was how the world was: full of surprises. In any case, what really made what he'd done for the Guantánamo men unusual wasn't the history between his country and the United States, but the fact of trying to help resolve another country's problems at all; it wasn't what nations usually did, the tendency being to always put one's own self-interest first, and on the one hand he could see the logic, you've got a certain amount of resources and your people rely on you to take care of their own interests with them, in poorer countries especially that's a paramount concern, sure, all right, but on the other hand no way, that logic won't hold, that model of leadership will be completely useless for the catastrophe ahead, because it's coming for everyone, climate change is coming for us all and it doesn't give a shit about our invented borders, nature isn't going to divide up the consequences of what's been done to it based on some sort of tit for tat of who did what before, so the whole model of who cleans up what has to change, and fast, the whole so-called Third World is going to have to—

"Do you think your own history may have helped you empathize with those men?"

A relief to be pulled from the flow of his own thoughts. He folded his palms in his lap, unfolded them. "In my case, sure. They suffered terribly in prison, and I know what that's like. But I hope that's not what it takes for other leaders to bring empathy to their role."

"Ah—" She looked startled. "Yes. What a thought." She stared down at her clipboard for a moment. "Tell me about the beginning."

His spine tensed. Here it came.

"When did you know you were going to run for president?"

She hadn't probed where he thought she would. He took a slow breath and looked out at the path to the vegetable garden with its tangled green. "Never. I'm still amazed."

She laughed, but her face was still serious. "The prison years didn't stop you."

"No." He paused, searching for a way to encapsulate what was going through his mind. "For a while, of course, I was stopped—there's only so much you can do from a hole in the ground. And I lost my mind for a while, as everybody knows"—here he hesitated, on the brink of saying more, of breaking open the story, why not talk about the frog, maybe he was wrong to think it couldn't be told, to think no one would ever understand; maybe this was the day to break the silence; of all the interviewers who'd come to see him, she seemed the one most likely to be able to receive. It was right there under the surface and her eyes conveyed that she was ready to hear anything, there it was, that dangerous thing, the listening gift—"but it got better in the later years, when I was allowed books. Reading saved my life. My mother could visit me by then too, and she brought me all the books she could. Science books, because the soldiers wouldn't allow anything else. I read them all, every word. I learned a lot of science."

He'd meant it earnestly, but she laughed. He laughed along with her. It was true things changed radically once he could read. Certainly there were no more shouting ants, no more conversations with frogs. He was far from the frog now, turning his attention to the later years, the book years, what followed.

"Then, after I got out, I devoted myself to rebuilding the country however I could, talking with people wherever I could, that was the only politics I knew."

"There's no one else with a story like yours," she said. "Wouldn't you say?"

A couple of dogs barked, playing, he thought, out by the vegetable garden. Angelita and one of the others. Fortunately there were no tractors around. "I'd say that's true about every single living person. No two people have the same trajectory. We all have our path through this world, not because it's destined, but because we shape it, we make it by walking, like that famous Machado poem says, and it's what's true. We make the road by walking and you can't always guess what's possible before it unfolds."

The reporter seemed to hover on the brink of several different questions, trying to decide on the best one.

Then she leaned back. "These, Mr. President, are very philosophical answers."

He smiled, saw the breeze had caught a strand of her hair, made it dance. So intent was her focus that she didn't seem to notice.

"What other kind of answer is there?" he said.

——

D own in the hole, the man tried to give the frog what he wanted: Once upon a time, he said, there was a group of young men and women who dreamed of justice. They looked around their beloved country and were wrenched by what they saw. Inequality. Workers who couldn't earn enough to eat, or for their children to eat, wages dropping as the price of food spiked. Families struggling to live. Foreign companies exploiting laborers and not caring about whether or not their families lived. And the government did not protect them. The government was not on their side. There were old people in these young people's communities who told stories of a gentler time when the government provided peace and care and order for the people, but those times were long gone and the young people questioned whether they'd ever existed at all or, if they had existed, whether the peace and care and order had been parceled out only to some and never to everyone, never to the dispossessed.

Their nation was still a democracy then. But even that word, *democracy*, seemed empty—you have to understand. Or maybe you won't understand, but I'll try to explain it anyway: hypocrisy can hollow a word out from the inside, gut it of meaning. There were elected leaders, all right, and those leaders took an oath, didn't they, to serve and represent the people? So what did it mean if they then used their positions of power to harm the people instead? And when the people rose up to protest and the elected leaders responded not by listening, but by sending armed police to attack ordinary citizens, what could that be called? A lie, a sham, a farce? A democracy gone bankrupt? A government-sponsored siege? Are the people then constituents, or hostages? Whom does such a democracy really serve?

You get my drift, I hope.

Meanwhile, all over the nation, children starved.

Some of the young men and women who dreamed came from laboring families and knew hunger in their own bones; others were radicalized at the university, down the hall from classrooms, at study sessions that digressed from impending exams to the realities of those less fortunate. All the young men, and all the young women, dreamed of something better for their people. I don't know that history will remember it that way, whether the school textbooks of the future will make them out as monsters or fools, I shudder to think of the textbooks the regime is churning out now—but let me tell you this, in this hole where no historian will ever hear me so it's probably pointless but what the hell: they were dreamers, it all started with a dream.

With a *What if*.

What if, they said, a country could share its resources equally enough so that all people have what they need to survive? What if workers had the right to decent pay? What if every child deserves a chance to learn, to eat, to be safe? What if our society respected all the people in it and not just the wealthy few? What if we had a conscience? What if there's another way? What if we could be governed by the principles of dignity and humanity, rather than exploitation, and what if those principles reached all the way into the halls of power? What if the halls of power could be shaken into newer, kinder forms? What if we could organize ourselves in a new manner, one dreamed of by visionary thinkers but never quite seen before? What if the people could actually lead themselves, or have leaders who genuinely worked on their behalf?

What if, what if, what if was the refrain of their great song.

They found their way to living rooms and cafés where people gathered to dream. They read Marx, discussed the future and the troubles of today, and found inspiration in what had happened in other countries throughout Latin America and the Caribbean, especially the Caribbean, especially one particular country in the Caribbean where revolution had liberated ordinary people, or so it was told, so the story went, and let me tell you, it was an intoxicating story, we got drunk on it, we swallowed it with all the ferocity of the parched, yes I said we, because of course I was there, I was in those meetings, first as a listener, then as a member, then as an organizer. We kept on telling stories, reading, dreaming. It wasn't hard for them to convert me, early on. It happened in an instant: all of a sudden, in the middle of listening to an organizer's report-back from the brutal sugarcane fields, I saw the gap between the world as it was, and the world as it should be. That gap was a wound. Suffering flowed from it. How could I rest until it healed? It was a lesion that had been opened on this continent in the days of the conquistadors;

perhaps, with luck and power, the healing would reach not only the living but many generations of the dead, not in some kind of heaven, because I was already an atheist by then, but just, I don't know, in memory, in the honoring and the finally setting to right.

On many nights after that, before falling asleep, I'd see the rising tides of Latin American revolutions, not just as an idea, but as an immense ocean wave cresting skyscraper high, full of faces, thousands of them, flecking the foam, gathering strength to sweep across the continent. We'd wash away generations of bloodshed, clean the wounds, flood communities with the healing balm of freedom. You can laugh, you can scoff, you can wonder about the weird logic of humans like me, but it's the truth, that's what revolution looked like to me when I gave my life to it: a balm.

Months passed. We kept dreaming, organizing. The labor strikes continued fiercely, with the government becoming more and more harsh in its response. The young men and women who dreamed of justice joined the strikes, the marches, the rallies outside of Parliament. They—we—saw the indifference of those in power. We saw that those who held the reins did not do so on behalf of the people, regardless of what the constitution might say, regardless of what they'd vowed on taking office.

They were against us, against the people. What else could explain the beating of peaceful protesters, the shooting into unarmed crowds, the horror stories of those who were arrested for marching, the blankness in their eyes on their return? But none of this stopped the demonstrations or the clandestine meetings. No. The fight broadened, deepened. It was a fight for survival, for the most basic of dignities, for human rights. The young men and women fought, and as they did, they watched things get worse: the economy collapsed, wages and jobs went up in smoke, government assistance was slashed, prices soared. Bread, milk, who could afford it? Where would it end? Protesters were gunned down; leaders were exposed as corrupt but kept on leading, and the journalists who'd exposed them started fearing for their lives. The young men and women lost their faith, regained it in new places. They dreamed. They read theory. They carried banners. They braved arrest. They burned for a more just future. Yes, for justice, which was, they declared, a form of love. They'd transform their nation into a nation of the people. They'd make it real, here in this country, make life better and more fair for the workers and their families, build a new kind of world together, fueled by the people's collective power, as forged by them, as channeled by them; and then a question arose before them like a hill in a green landscape: if it had to be done, if they were the ones to do it, then—armed struggle, yes or no?

No.

Yes.

No.

Some answered this. Some answered that.

Some balked at the idea of armed struggle, held to visions of another way.

But others, drawing on examples of revolutions around the world, said, look, this is the necessary path, the only viable one. The government is too corrupt for change to ever come from its own hands, they'll never allow it. They will always defend the status quo no matter how many lives the status quo destroys.

If we build power—through elections—

Elections! Revolution through elections? No.

Impossible.

But why?

Don't make me laugh.

If we could—

You don't see it? The system is too far gone. Politicians are invested in the structures of power as they stand, and if not them, then the Empire that backs them from up North will make sure they stay in line no matter how much it means hurting their own people.

I don't want to believe that.

Too bad.

So you're saying, what, then? That we have to take up arms?

I'm saying the only way is to rise up on behalf of the people and claim the power the people deserve.

That was how it started. With fierce debates in secret gathering spaces, such as, for me, a small shed in a cobbler's backyard where a bottle of wine made the rounds, each of us taking swigs in turn, swigs of wine, swigs of reasoning, all of it merging inside our skins. Some people split off from the group after that, but many stayed and so did I. What can I tell you? There was power in the dream. If words could make a dream come true we would have transformed the continent with those nights. Instead we founded a movement, a new movement, an armed movement, and we risked everything, gave everything, gambled it all, hurled ourselves relentlessly onto the path toward that bright new day and let me tell you, in this story, those armed revolutionaries over the years had some triumphs but also made some mistakes, oh yes we did, more than I'd like to admit but, look, the movement wasn't perfect; it was a hard road, a wild road, and toward the end it spun beyond our control. We weren't prepared for the fast growth of later years as our successes became

known and our popularity grew among the common people, we were called a band of Robin Hoods because we
stole from casinos to give food to the poor, held up banks
and passed out toys in the slums on holidays, as well as,
of course, using that same booty to stockpile weapons for
the revolution to come (and come it would, we thought,
throughout the globe, even the heart of Empire had its
own uprising! the Black Panthers! and we cheered for
them, from far down south, our brothers and sisters in
the struggle), all of which gave us a reputation that, in our
heyday, brought eager idealists to us in droves, disgusted
by government crackdowns and thrilled by our small vic-
tories, thinking one day they'd tell their grandkids how
they won the country for the masses. Well. All that fast
growth in the middle of crackdowns, it wasn't easy. We
weren't prepared. And how to keep order in the rank and
file when you're operating in deepest secrecy, when your
best and brightest are ground under the torturer's wheel
and then spit back out into your lap? The systems we'd
created were strong and unseen, like a spider's web, and
I'm sure you know all about spiders' webs, you've probably crawled around and under them many times, perhaps even seeking out your dinner, so you know what I'm
about to say is true: spider threads are incredibly strong,
but not impossible to break. Not at all. There were more

ups and downs and waves of hope and crushing than I care to tell you. Suffice to say that, after years of struggle, we ultimately found ourselves indeed in a different world, but not the justice world we'd dreamed of, nope, rather in a world that was not better but unfathomably worse.

Was it our fault?

I say no. I must say no. Most days I believe it even though they've managed to crush so much of what I've believed.

I can't hear any other answer.

Others blame us, I know, I know. God knows what the censored press is saying now.

Our presence may have played a role in the collapse that brought us to this place, and that wrenches me more than I could ever say.

Still.

It's so easy to blame the broken.

So frightening to blame the fist of power.

Back to how it was for us, at the end. For the men and women who'd dreamed.

Fog closed in on every side, we couldn't see.

The fist tightened.

The torture chambers destroyed thousands of souls.

Now there was no more air to breathe.

The End.

P*erky, that one!*
"You wanted more story. That's got more story than the one before."
So you're giving up on the world, eh?
"The world gave up on us."
Coward.
"How can you call me that?"
It's easy, watch. Coward! Coward!
"You little son of a bitch. You don't know what I've been through."
So what. No one knows what anyone else has been through.
To this the future president had no ready response.
You won't go back for anyone?
"I can't go back. I'm trapped here."
But if you could?
He could only answer with the way he felt this instant, for the instants were all different, nothing was solid, nothing guaranteed. "No."

Not even for a female?

"I said no."

But don't you have a female?

"A girlfriend, is that what you mean? Yes, sure."

Tell me about her.

"Shut up."

Come on, you have to give me more. Tell me about the female.

"Let's talk about something else. I'll come up with another story. Anything except her."

Why?

"None of your goddamn business."

All right! Touchy!

"And while we're at it, this *female* thing is bullshit. That's not how we are. Were. In the movement, I mean. Women were treated with respect, not like that at all."

Female is not respect?

"You don't get it. You're an animal, what do you know? Sorry, I love animals, what am I saying? I didn't mean it as an insult. Or—hm. If I did, I can see I was out of line."

Hum.

"What I mean is, yes, to us humans it's dismissive and I don't like you talking about her that way."

Hum-hum.

"You don't believe me? What's your problem?"

Aha! Riled up again, we are.

"That's because—"

Good. Be riled, be wakeup.

"That doesn't make— Sorry, I forgot again, you don't give a crap about sense. Anyway. I was talking about something, it was important—oh yes, women. We had a different kind of code, a better one, the revolution was for all of us, men and women too. Liberation for all. Our movement had strong women fighters."

As many as men?

"Uh—well, no, of course not. I mean, all right, the leaders were male. But the women were there too, and they mattered, they taught us a great deal, we protected them, worked with them. They were important to us, because people were less suspicious of them, they could come off as more innocent so they did great undercover. And they knew how to use their voices. There was this one young woman in the movement, she rose up the ranks, she even made it into central command, she was that good at all the things she did, and once in the early days she stomped out of a meeting and came back with a mustache painted on her face, and you know what she said? She boomed it, in an exaggeratedly deep voice. Now will you listen to me? We hadn't realized we hadn't been listening to her, hadn't noticed her attempts to cut in, and now she looked adorable with her lush hair and tight blouse and that mustache painted on. It made us laugh. It made us want her. At that point she had all of our attention, I can tell you, we'd completely forgotten our discussion. Only when the laughter died down did we see how serious her face was, how intense. We got quiet then and let her talk. I can't remember what she told us, but we all listened at the time, and after that she never had to paint a mustache on again. You see?" It was meant to be a funny story, and the man had laughed about it with his comrades many times, but now the frog was silent and a sticky heat ran through him as he recalled what he'd thought had been a tale of respect for women, meant to prove the equality in their movement, an assertion of which he was suddenly less sure.

Ho-de-ho, hm.

"I don't know why I talk to you."

I do.

"You think you know everything about everything but you don't, you're part of this hole, you don't know a damn thing about the world."

The world is here.

"What?"

Here, here, the world is this hole.

"That's ridiculous."

Here hole here hole heeeeeeere—

And then the frog was gone.

That night, in the hole, the man dreamed. His nation was a woman, bound and blindfolded, naked on a cold floor. Blood spread down her thighs. Over her, a figure in uniform, with bushy hair and garish teeth. He leers, drunk on raping, still hungry. And he too is the nation. The image tips, twists, distorts. Two bodies, one nation. What the man can't know, what he can't tell, what's lost in the blurred mist is where the nation will ultimately live, in the body in uniform or the naked body on the ground or somewhere else, in the charge between them, the shattered dance.

‑‑➤‑‑◄‑

It was a dream, he told himself when his eyes jerked open, body cold with sweat. It was just a dream.

But it was late for that. The borders had blurred, the walls between waking and dreamscape had melted, and there was no room in the hole for their separation.

—>—<—

M any people in Europe," the reporter said, "find it incredible that you took the helm of the same government that once treated you so brutally."

"Well," the ex-president said. He took a breath. Angelita had tired of her play out by the vegetables and come to curl up at his feet, where she now dozed. He stroked her gently with the side of his foot, took solace in her warmth. The things he did to keep Angelita warm: in the winter, she'd wake him three and even four times in the night, begging for another log in the woodstove, and he'd comply, even when he was in the middle of running the country, why not, pass a law, take a meeting, put another log on the fire during a cold winter night, stroke your dog by the glow of that fire, all in the work of a day and its ensuing night. *Don't wear yourself out,* his wife might murmur from the bed, *you've got another long day ahead tomorrow,* but she wouldn't push it; she understood. There were days when you could not get the Senate or a foreign leader or the general public to see things your way, days when the patient machinations necessary for keeping all the factions happy could drive you to the edge of despair, days when all the problems of your country writhed on your shoulders in relentless knots and it seemed criminal, how little you could do even from your presidential status to ease the people's pain (and how can it be, you'd think, how can it be, that I'm the person with the most power in this entire country, having reached the top rung of the ill-famed ladder only to find that there's so very much you still can't do, could never pull off, never accomplish, not even if the people's will is behind you, because your country's power isn't just about your own people, it's about the great web of power woven inextricably across the globe, an international tangle of unseen threads that hold realities together, hold economies together, you are enmeshed, you are beholden, you couldn't see the full extent of that web of power before you reached the ladder's top and now it's clear as day to you but still invisible for the most part to the people except as an oppression from which they demand to be freed, and sure, yes, they deserve to be free, you've fought all your life for that very thing and absolutely nothing else, but what you see from this vantage point is the devilish complexity of power's tangle, cut this strand and that other strand will collapse until next thing you know there's no bread left for anyone, so you try to protect the people's bread and free them at the same time, and the people talk, the people shout, he should do more, why doesn't he act, a few even throw around the word *sellout,* and there you are on that narrow top rung doing all you can, which is not enough, still and always and forever not enough) and after days like that what better medicine could there be than making warmth for Angelita and meeting the love in Angelita's eyes? None, that was the answer. None at all. "Life is full of twists and turns," he said.

"The people were ready to support you, despite your past, or perhaps in part because of it?"

The ex-president sighed. "There was a little bit of everything," he said, remembering his first term in the Senate, when senior colleagues had muttered about having to serve alongside *that dirty guerrilla,* without even bothering to move out of earshot or keep their voices down. Those had been tense days, after the first wave of ex-guerrillas rode into the halls of Congress, but they'd been heady days too because they'd known, even then, that it was just the beginning, the first gathering of a rising crest, a shifting of the underlying language of power that was only getting started. "But during the campaign

I was completely open so the public wouldn't be caught off guard. I laid it all out from the beginning: this is who I am, where I've come from, how my attempts to serve my country have looked at different times. And sure, yes, at one point it involved trying to overthrow the government, not join it. Humm. What can I say? It was another era. The outlook was different, but the aim has always been the same: to help the people of this country. To lift the country up, make it a better place for everyone. That was the intention. We didn't always meet it. Our movement was far from perfect." They'd been wrong about some things, right about others, and he'd spend decades parsing which broken shards belonged where, in the right, in the wrong, they slipped, they collided, shards in raucous chaos, jumbling the mosaic of the past. "I'd tell people that if they hated what we did back then, I'd understand, and it didn't matter to me. What matters is what's right for today. Back then, in the guerrilla days, we thought we couldn't achieve meaningful change with electoral politics." He was thinking aloud now, he realized; he'd always loved to think aloud, finding his way along the thread of speech like Theseus in the labyrinth, and though becoming president had meant people by his side constantly warned him to think before he spoke, he sometimes did, sometimes didn't. "Now, it's clear we can't have meaningful change without it."

"Without . . . electoral politics?"

"Right."

"These are some of the things you said in your campaign?"

"Yes."

"And people heard you?"

"Apparently, some did."

She laughed a little. The air seemed to lift and warm around them. He hadn't meant to be funny, or maybe he had but without knowing it; the line in his mind between humor and gravity was often razor thin, invisible to his own inner eye.

"It's still a conversation," he said. "And that's how it should be. Society is one long unending conversation. The thing is, in our country, there are very few people who don't carry scars from the bad times. They were everyone's bad times, even if people carry them in different ways, even if my wounds are more obvious than some."

"Because everyone was affected?"

"That's right."

"A national trauma."

"Exactly."

"Does it make a society stronger, in some way? Having been through something harrowing together?"

"Ah." He spread his hands apart, held them open. "That depends."

"On what?"

"On the society."

The reporter's gaze became searching. A flicker of something—sorrow or fear or piercing worry—swept across her face. "I see your point." She tucked her hair behind her left ear; it was a habit of hers, he realized, an unconscious gesture, and he wondered how she used it, to smooth discomfort, perhaps, or muster courage, or help her think. "I can't imagine what it would be like, in your position, to work with the military. After what they did."

The ex-president leaned forward slightly. He wondered whether he'd been wrong about her age; she seemed younger now, despite her poise, in her late thirties or so, and she could be his grandchild, a thought that seared him with a pure, surprising tenderness. "I went to them the day after my inauguration. To assure them that the new government would support them too."

"Wasn't that"—she searched for the right word—"difficult?"

"Not really. Or if it was, that wasn't the thing that mattered." What a morning that had been. Light had filled the dining hall, draped his podium and the national flag on the far wall as well as the clean-shaven faces stretched out in rows before him, and the truth was that he'd felt afraid, of course he had, he'd girded himself for waves of grief or rage or flashbacks at the sight of so many uniformed men, but once he got to the podium all that struck him was amazement at how young some of those faces were, how fresh to life even in their suspicion of the stout man at the podium. These boys weren't his captors, had never had the chance, some of them hadn't even been born yet in the bad old days. Still. That didn't mean they weren't biased; they'd probably come of age hearing guerrillas were the closest thing to demons in this world. And then he'd won them over. Many of them, anyway. Talk as magic. He told them the truth, that they were important to the country, that it was his job to serve them as they too were the people of this land. "It's a question of priorities. I came in with a mandate to help create good jobs and alleviate poverty and inequality—you know, to improve people's lives. That was more important than grudges. That was more important than whether or not a meeting would be personally hard for me." Those early days. A blur of talk and work and the word *president* gliding close around his head, as improbable as ever, brushing against his scalp with unseen wings. "In fact, in my first months in office, I went in the opposite direction. I tried to soften the sentences of the small handful of generals serving prison time for their dictatorship-era crimes. If I'd had my way, they would have been able to move from their bleak cells to house arrest."

"Really? You would have forgiven them?"

"Not forgiveness. Just a level of humanity. What's the point of keeping old men in cells? What does it change?" Some of those generals had been the very ones to orchestrate his own suffering, had given the detailed orders, and that wasn't conjecture, it had all come to light now and was widely known. And yet he'd surprised himself by harboring no rancor, no need for revenge. Why not? He wasn't sure, but it had something to do with urgency. Rancor and revenge could keep you mired in the past, a swamp of which he wished to be free; he couldn't afford that sort of thing, there was too much to do in the here and now. Age helps clarify such matters. In his youth, the illusion of infinite time might have tempted him to cling to rage along with all the other fires, but by the time he entered the presidency—for that's how it felt, more than becoming president: *entering* the presidency, as if it were an edifice that had been standing in the same place for generations, not something you became at all, but a space you inhabited for a time and made your tenuous, overly grand, temporary yet soul-defining home—by that time he was already an old man and had to choose where his vitality would go. At his inauguration, he was seventy-five years old, acutely aware that vitality was finite, as was time. There would never be enough of either. Therefore, he'd only spend his vitality and time on whatever was best for the nation, and the nation needed a good relationship with its military, at least good enough to prevent thoughts of a coup; a show of goodwill could go a long way toward being shown goodwill in turn, and what mattered was the future, for the promise of the slogan Never Again so often heard throughout Latin America—first about the Holocaust, now about the Holocaust as well as the horrors of dictatorships and disappearances—to actually be kept. But he lost that one. The battle for leniency toward regime generals was one of the many he lost. Too many people on the left wanted the harshest possible treatment for those men, so he'd calculated the energy such a fight would call for, weighed it against other pressing fights, and let the matter go. "I still believe it would have been a good strategy, thinking for the future. But it didn't come to pass."

"Most people in your shoes would want to see those men suffer as much as possible."

ened somehow, by something—what? laughter? insults?
the frog?

Talk to me.

The invitation was irresistible, why deny it, and yet he
dallied, wouldn't let on. He wanted to stretch time, not
give in easily, toy with the request. And then he thought,
what have I come to, acting coy with a frog. "Don't tell
me it's story time."

It's always story time.

"No, it's not!"

Then what else is there?

"Well, not much else in here, but out in the world
there's fighting time, work time, sex time, sleep time,
planting time, organize-for-the-movement time—"

All story times.

"You're nuts."

And are you.

"Huh? So what? I mean, who isn't, anyway? How about
the people running this dungeon, can you really call them
sane? And the people they report to and the people above
that? What are we supposed to call it when the people in
power who are supposed to serve the people turn around
and attack them instead?"

Tell me what you call it.

"Corruption! Injustice! A machine to grind the people,

that's all the government is. That's why we were going to overthrow it, to claim it on behalf of the people."

That went just dandy.

"Yeah. I know. You've made that point, and I don't want to tell that part again."

There's the other side of it.

"What other side?"

That even if you'd won—you see the problem.

"Problem? No, that would have been great, what problem?"

The problem of after.

"After what? The revolution? We would have been different, we had a whole plan, the leadership had it all mapped out. How we'd shape the new government, start over, build our society afresh. We'd expropriate land so even the humblest families would have soil to till and food to eat, make sure all the workers had dignity, choose new leaders and keep them accountable to the people, the lot of it, what do you think we were, amateurs?"

And that would have worked?

"Absolutely."

The way your fighting plans worked?

"Low blow."

I am always low. I am nowhere else.

"Low to the ground?"

To the groundy ground.

"Good God."

Which god?

"There is no God, it's a figure of speech. Anyway, you know what I mean."

It is yours, the saying of what you mean.

"Well, what I'm saying is, regardless of how our fighting plans went—and the fall was *not* our fault, we were crushed, the Yankee Empire sent its henchmen and destroyed us, all right?—this postrevolution plan would actually have worked."

How do you know?

"I know."

You don't know.

"Neither do you, so go to hell."

Where is hell?

"There is no hell, I don't believe in all that Catholic propaganda, I just said there is no God and that's the deal. No God, no hell. This is hell, this hole right here. Although, hmm. That means I just sent you to—"

—right here.

"Yes."

Aha-dida!

"Damn. Hey. What if, in some other dimension, some other man in a hole told you to go to hell, and you did, and you vanished and ended up here?" He laughed. It made his ribs hurt, but he couldn't help it, couldn't stop, the pleasure of it was worth the pain. "I think I read something like that once, in a Borges story. It would certainly explain how you got here." Much more sensible, he thought, than his nightmarish imagining of a network of spy-frogs; anything that sounded like a Borges story had to be at least half-true, and this he would have said long before the hole, when he was a young guy devouring books at the National Library, swallowing tales that swallowed him in turn and showed him the real world anew.

This is not where we were.

"So?"

I am opening the question.

"Huh? What question?"

Do you know how you would lead?

"Lead what—the movement?"

No. The country. If you were the leader of your country.

He snorted. "Well, that's impossible now."

You barely know the ocean of the possible.

"That's a mean thing to say to someone in"—he gestured vaguely at the walls, at his body—"my situation. In here, there's no ocean of anything."

Not that you can see.

"Any different from what *you* see?"

I don't have blind in your human way.

"No, I guess not, you only *have* blind in your frog-way. Much better, I'm sure, you pest."

Now now, calling names, what is this?

"All right, that was too much. You're not a pest—or not only a pest. I told you before, I love animals and I meant it. Truth is, this land belongs to you more than to the soldiers clomping around up there, or to me."

You're stalling. And you're hiding from my question.

"You had a question?"

How would you lead?

He scratched his thigh. In fact, the question prickled him. Against his will he heard his mother cooing over him as she dried his limbs fresh from the bath, brushed his hair for school, *My son, my boy, my angel-boy, you can be anything, you can be president, you'll see, you'll show the world*—but it stabbed him to hear his mother's voice inside this place, and so, as always when his mind roamed toward her, he shut off the thought and shrank away. He could not bear to linger on thoughts of Mamá, to whom he'd never had the chance to say goodbye, whose pain over his absence had to be ferocious beyond imagining. She'd probably been searching for him with every ounce of her strength. He could picture her storming into every

conceivable government building with his birth certifi-
cate and identification photo in her purse, seeking clues
as to his whereabouts, being forced to wait for hours,
being told nothing, coming back the next day anyway
because that was how his mother was, she wouldn't give
up, which meant her suffering these past four years had
surely been relentless. How he'd failed her. All that hope
she'd put into the bathing, the brushing, the caring for
her little you-can-be-anything boy, and here he was, in
this bleak hole. "I told you. It's too late for that."

Late, late, early late, so late you end up early . . .

"Oh god, not your singing again."

Cowardy man, has no plan, cannot stand . . .

"Damn you to hell."

There is no hell. The words from you.

"Good point. Touché. Although, I also said this was
hell right here."

Then you have sent me and here I am.

"That makes my head hurt. You know what, let's talk
about something else."

About the female?

"Stop calling her that. I already told you."

*Oh yes, of course, revolution! Respect! Female is not
respect! Mustache respect! Blah blah!*

"You're a son of a bitch."

But you haven't said her name.

"Sofía. Her name is Sofía."

Sofííííaaaaaa—

"My God, what an ugly singing voice you have."

Tell me of her or I'll keep singing.

He opened his mouth to refuse, but something caved inside him and before he knew it he was speaking. "She was beautiful. Is beautiful. I mean I don't know what they've done to her but they can't take that away." Which, he thought against his will, might not be strictly true; who knew what they were capable of doing to a body; but even then there was much more than how a body looked, she was lit up from the inside, she had a spark that caught him like a moth and that he still believed (or was it hoped?) no torturer would have been able to extinguish and so yes, damn it, she was still beautiful no matter what. Even if—but what if—

She was a guerrilla too?

"Yes. And a fierce one."

And?

"And—" He struggled against the images that flooded him, of what they might have done to her, of how she might be now, railing against them and hurling himself back in time toward an earlier incarnation of Sofía as she was before the fall, ready for action, brave and able, a curvy Wonder Woman in ordinary clothes with a pistol at the hip of her trousers, her face a wall of determination even when all seemed lost. Sofía. Sofía the natural leader, who'd graced him with her time, her skin, her ferocious mind, the blaze in her eyes when she said *revolution*. Sofía of the blaze.

Story, said the frog. *Now the story.*

—➤—◀—

Once upon a time there was a group of revolutionaries who'd dreamed of changing the world for the better by fighting the forces of repression, but the forces of repression were a monster that grew new tentacles with every battle they fought. The war grew epic, out of proportion to the size of their own country. The guerrillas watched their comrades get gunned down in the streets, in their homes, be captured and tortured and vilified in the press, on television and radio shows where censors magnified the missteps of the guerrillas—which, granted, did exist—and glossed over the far greater crimes of the government forces. Meanwhile, they also lost another vital resource: the support of public opinion. They'd thought the people would be on their side and rise up with them when the time came. They'd thought, we'll lead, they'll gladly follow. But then the guerrillas turned around and saw they were alone. The people were tired. They were scared. They watched the television news reports of shoot-outs in the streets and dangerous subversives and they wanted an end to it all. Looking back at it this way, who could blame them? Still. Gone were the days when the public had cheered for a movement known for robbing from rich institutions to give to the poor, for stockpiling guns, yes, but for a revolution that was in all of their names, who— All right, look, I know you've heard some of this before, I realize I may be getting a little repetitive, but it's important to me and in any case I swear I'm getting to the girlfriend, all right? It's coming, don't worry, calm down.

Anyway. We were losing, and we were alone. The walls were caving in on us from all sides. We'd hidden in cellars, down trapdoors, in sheds, more cellars, and, finally, we were running out of places and ended up in a woodsy park at the outskirts of the city, I took my ragged group there under cover of night, I could have gotten there blindfolded—and by then I'd already been tortured so, believe me, I knew all about blindfolds—because it was not so far from where I grew up and that little forest was a good cover. The catch was, it was June. The last days of autumn. Biting cold at night and we couldn't light a fire for fear of being discovered. Our hands and ears ached from the cold.

And one night, it was Sofía keeping watch.

She'd been quiet at that evening's meeting. Her boyfriend had recently been gunned down by the police.
It wasn't like her to stay out of discussions, she usually
brightened them and kept them afloat. I knew it was the
grief though she wouldn't say it aloud, determined to be a
strong guerrilla and take it in stride; the movement needed
her to keep it together so keep it together she would. I'd
admired her for years. Dreamed of her, wanted her from
afar—many of our comrades had—but she'd always
been spoken for, wrapped up with the partner who had
just been killed. In another universe, in another history,
she would have been off-limits while she mourned, but
we were far beyond the world where limits could exist,
of the off kind or the on. That night, we sat close when
the others, the younger guerrillas, were asleep. Talked.
We were the two veteran fighters in our group—she was
younger than me, but still older than most at thirty years
old—and the talking was a comfort, different from talking to newer recruits, who looked to you for guidance
and encouragement. You couldn't show the young ones
all the chaos in your soul. But with Sofía, there was no
need to hide the chaos or the sorrow or even the blind
pain, and no use trying anyway; without saying a word
we could feel it in each other, accompany each other's
secret thoughts. It had been years since my last girlfriend

had broken up with me, back when I was locked up at that city prison, she couldn't take the pressure and in truth I could see why. She wasn't a guerrilla, hadn't even known I was one when she took up with me, hadn't signed up for that kind of life and—who could blame her—it was more than she could bear. By now, that night in the forest, I was thirty-seven years old and with the state of things I'd given up on having a girlfriend or a lover ever again. My life was for the revolution, so be it, fine, I'd hand it all over the way monks handed their lives over to God. Of course there are differences between monks and us, for one thing there's the fact no one sees subversives as holy, at least not once the movement starts going badly, at that point you're met with fear and revulsion, blamed for the collapse of the world. But still. The point is, it was as if I'd taken vows of chastity, or so I thought until that night in the urban forest with Sofía. Our bodies spoke to each other without touching for a long time. We whispered about one thing and another, everything except her dead boyfriend or what we were doing in that forest that night or what the future held for us. I told her stories of my childhood, low, under my breath, made her laugh. I wanted to court her the way you court a queen, with gems and treasures, only as a radical socialist I didn't believe in capitalist gems and treasures nor did I have any, I barely had a peso, all I had were my words and whatever my words could hold. We went on like this until finally she looked up at me and I looked back and as we held each other's gaze I saw she was formidable, that she was no less formidable than me. Even now in her grief I could see it. I'd suspected as much about her for years and now it was laid bare. I saw the rest of it too. Fear. Sorrow. Knowledge of the end. None of which we spoke about but we didn't have to. You know what, she said, the only refuge left is what we give each other. I felt as though I could drown in her eyes, and that was all I wanted to do. Just drown and let the whole damn world vanish forever. But I couldn't do that. The young ones needed me. So instead I said, I can't imagine a better refuge than you. She looked amused. Really? she said. That's the best you've got? It's what I've got tonight, I said. And with all the stories I heard about you, she said. Stories, I said, what stories? And that's when she kissed me. We kissed for a long time as our hands dove under each other's clothes to flee the cold. Danger had been part of my life for a long time now, I'd been living underground with false IDs for years, but that night was different. My God, I thought as I buried a hand in her hair, we met in the wrong life, if only we'd met in a more peaceful time and place, with years before us instead of this, what we could have been.

We made love as if it were the last chance in our lives. The next night we made love the same way, and the next night, and the next, and the nights extended in that forest into weeks, every night unpromised, served up cold and fragile as the revolution shattered slowly all around us.

By the time I was taken, Sofía was in me, how else can I put it, and it seemed I was also in her. Don't look at me like that, that's not what I mean and this is no time for vulgarity, I'm trying to tell you something. You can be as vulgar as you want about me but not about her, I'll knock your clammy little block off.

Within hours of my capture, I learned that she'd been captured too.

And what was done to her has to have been worse than what was done to me—all the things they do to men they do to women, and also more. An unspeakable more. And that's what really makes me hate the world, makes me want to leave the world, abandon it to whatever jerks will have it, push off from sanity like the big fucked-up lie it is—the thought of them breaking her, destroying what was so completely alive.

The frog was silent.

The man waited but nothing came. The ache in his limbs rose to roaring in the silence.

"Well?" he finally said. "Nothing to say?"

That's dumb.

"What? You ingrate, you don't deserve a story like that if—"

Not the whole story. That last part. It's a dumb thought, when you don't even know.

"Know what?"

Whether she's broken.

The image from the dream arose, the blindfolded figure on the floor, she had Sofía's hair, Sofía's shoulders, how could he have missed that before? Perhaps because he hadn't wanted to see it. Was that all it took for people's minds to protect them from what they knew? "How can she not be broken? How can any of us not be?"

You don't want to be broken, don't be broken.

"You're a frog. You don't know what humans do to each other—what they've done to us."

And what they haven't done.

"There's nothing they haven't done. Just look at me. They've starved me, beaten me, tortured me with their fancy imported torture machines, put me here alone, and done it not just to me but to the lot of us, the resistance lost, we're lost, we're all done for."

Ho-de-dum, co-co-comes a sto-rm.

"Have you even been listening?"

Silly man.

"Fuck you."

The frog hopped away, toward the shadows.

"Wait. Don't go."

You don't want me here.

"I do. I'm lonely. Stay."

The frog hopped back, halfway, seemed to wait.

"Please stay," he said, more gently this time. "I hurt your feelings?"

Acha acha, you know nothing.

"Not true."

You can't see your own story.

"Just the opposite. My problem is I see it all too well." Except, he thought to himself, when you're caught by the static interference in your brain, then you're scrambled, man, you know you are, admit it, though right this second that's all mercifully dialed down, which is another reason to keep the frog close.

If you could see it you would know where you are inside the telling. You would know the difference between the end and The End.

"Hmmm, so, and what else? Dirt isn't dirt, shit isn't shit, a hole isn't a hole?"

Yes.

"That was a rhetorical—"

And also if you could see it you would find the One Thing.

"Eh? What's the One Thing?"

The thing you need.

"I don't know whether you've noticed, but I'm a wreck. I need a whole lot more than one thing. I mean, just look at me." He hadn't actually seen himself in years, could only imagine how he looked, sunken, emaciated, he didn't want to know. "I could use soap, water, a bed, a steak, a book, a phone, a crapper, a pen—God, don't make me choose between a crapper and a pen—"

There is One. In the One is All.

"Huh. The pen is a crapper? What is this, some sort of Swiss Army knife toilet with a—"

No. It's inside you.

"I hope we're not still talking about a crapper."

We were never talking that.

"Fine, great."

Inside is all.

"That's bullshit."

You have to find it.

"Find what?"

The One Thing.

"The One Thing. The damn One Thing. What the hell, man, I can't take it, can we talk about something else?"

Like?

"Tell me more about the surrounding land. What you see when you leave this damn place."

No.

"Not for an escape route—that's absurd, I know, I've let that go, I swear. I just need to hear about the outside world."

The frog stared at the future president for a long time, as if gathering intricate thoughts. *Green and green and living. Green and green and dirt.*

"Mmmmmm. Yes. I love dirt."

You do?

"Don't you remember my story about the prison escape? Becoming the worm?"

Worm, worm, guerrilla worm.

"Exactly. Through the dirt, which is everything. Dirt

may as well be my God. All the green living things rise from dirt and from it comes all life."

I thought there was no God?

"Still true. But if there were one, if I could choose one, it would be nature. Dirt. The earth."

This is where we need to go.

"What do you mean, go?"

For the One Thing you need.

"It's in the dirt? Are you fucking kidding me? For this famous One Thing, this ultra mystery, we're supposed to go scratching in the dirt?"

Not scratching. Telling. The reason for telling. The reason you give stories.

"I do it because you tell me to."

No. Not only.

"What else?" To keep the static down, the ants at bay. To not die or long to die.

There's a memory far down inside you and it's small but it holds everything you need.

"How can that be?"

It is One.

"Bah." The idea was insane, and he knew it, he was just sane enough to see when an idea had flung off the cliff; but then again, he couldn't see any good reason to keep clinging to sanity, which was a crumbling landscape anyway, no longer separate from the void beyond, so why not leap, why not hurl yourself out toward the melted territories where logic broke open and took new unmapped forms. Why not search for it, for this One Thing, if nothing else as a sort of diversion, a game to murder time. "So how the fuck do we find it?"

Begin.

"But where?"

Go to the places of before.

·>-·<·

Before.
    In another time.
    Once upon a time there was a kid who had no father. His father had died when he was seven years old, of syphilis, though this last part he would not fully understand until he was older, the reason his mother's grief mixed with a sense of betrayal, why a bright strand of anger tangled up his mother's sorrow. Why she'd sometimes say *he left us* rather than *he died*. For the boy, in the early years, the loss was pure, a grief rooted in incomprehension, how could it possibly be that his father would never again preside over Sunday lunch in the shade of the grapevine on their back patio, complimenting his wife's cooking and laughing conspiratorially with his only son as if they shared a marvelous secret, and always the boy would laugh along and wonder what the marvelous secret could be. He never found out. His father died and Sunday lunches became hollow, void of laughter. It was more

than that, too: without his father's income, the family had to strain to survive. Every day a battle. He watched his mother plant vegetables in the garden, in every corner of the soil, so they would have something to eat when pesos ran low, and he and his sister kneeled in the dirt beside her and learned how to work the land. His sister was too little to do more than scoop dirt into swirling mounds; it was he, at eight, at nine, who was the older one, responsible for the garden, for the family. He watched the dirt miraculously give rise to potatoes, tomatoes, carrots, bell peppers, squash, saw the way hours of digging and planting and weeding and watering translated over time into food. He went to school with dirt under his fingernails, no matter how much his mother insisted he get all the way clean, he tried his best and scrubbed and scrubbed but dirt was seeping into his hands and world. While other children climbed trees and kicked a ball around after school, he worked, and look, I know you know exactly who this kid is, no big mystery here, it's me, but still this is the way I'm going to tell it, all right? This is the way I can find. So. The kid started working first at a local bakery, in exchange for a few coins and bread to take home for his mother and sister to eat. That was the first job, and it went on for a while; after that there was never a time he wasn't working for pesos after school, and by the time he was in high school he was growing and selling flowers, carrying them on the bus in the mornings and selling them to florists near his school so as to have enough coins for the bus ride back. Sometimes, there wasn't enough money for his bus ride, and he'd borrow a coin or two from the baker he used to work for. He always made enough to repay the baker and carry some bread home. It wasn't water to wine, but flowers to bread. He became known on the bus as the young man with the flowers; soon he saw an opportunity to sell the blooms directly on the ride. He could sell as much as his arms could hold. That was how well he did. And let me tell you, he wasn't about to pass up such a chance, that's not the kind of kid he was. He loaded himself up with flowers, boarded the bus in an explosion of color. Housewives and grandmothers, especially, wanted his wares, chatted with him, laughed at his jokes and blushed at his compliments. He talked and sold and gave out smiles for free. Charm was everything, he learned. You had to charm when it came to flowers, or you were dead in the water. Flowers were joy at its most bright and fleeting. Who wanted to buy them from a depressed face? Fortunately, he was not depressed. He was full of the irrepressible energy of the young. He needed places to pour that energy. He poured it into selling flowers, chatting up buyers, reading books, biking with his best friend and relishing the wind as their wheels devoured the country roads, embarking on a short-lived time at the university, finding new places to sell flowers (open-air markets, cemetery gates), reading more books, dreaming his way onto the deck of Odysseus's ship, falling in love with Quixote and then Sancho and Quixote all over again, listening to his professors for hours in downtown cafés and especially the Spaniard who'd arrived in this country fleeing Franco after fighting in the Civil War (his tales of resistance would swim in the young man's head for years), listening to the meat workers as they organized their strike, helping the meat workers organize their strike, receiving gifts of meat wrapped in paper as thanks for helping with the strike, watching his mother cook that meat and thinking about the workers who'd carved it, listening to stories of solidarity with other workers, engaging in solidarity with other workers, meeting the sugarcane laborers who traveled from the northern reaches of the country to protest on the capital's main avenue, devouring socialist and communist theory, meeting the man who'd organized the sugarcane workers and had enormous dreams of liberation for the nation, allowing himself to get drunk on those enormous dreams of liberation as the wine and yerba mate made their rounds, swirling ever closer to the spark that would flare up into a revolutionary movement destined—so he thought—to transform his nation into a beautiful one where all kids, fatherless or not, had bread and books and all good things.

➤➤◄◄

T*hat's well and fine, but that's not it.*
"And how was I supposed to know?"
You moved too quickly across time.
"Hmm."
You skipped things.
"Of course I skipped things. That's the only way to tell a life without taking a whole life to do it. You pick the things that are most important to tell."
No.
"Uh—no?"
There is also slowing.
"What the hell is slowing?"
Also, you picked wrong.
"Oh yeah? I suppose frogs know better how to shoot the breeze? You know what, maybe it's your turn, you haven't told me any of your stories, now that I think about it. Why don't you talk about your side for a change,

your mama frog, your poor papa frog, who maybe died when you were however old you frogs are when you're kids—"

We're not getting anywhere.

"Whose fault is that? I don't know where we're going."

We'll go nowhere at this rate.

"We're already nowhere."

Yes, but it's the wrong nowhere.

"So there's a right one?"

Stay in the early now.

"Huh? You mean—mornings?"

Tell me from when you were boy.

At this, he tightened up inside, though he couldn't have said why. It must be night; the shaft of light was gone and dark shrouded the hole. A cave of dark. The frog was a patch of shadow inside of shadow. He'd just been talking about his boyhood, hadn't he? Now he stood accused of moving through it too fast. Was it true? Were there things he'd slid past that he didn't want to touch? If so, he wasn't about to let on. "That makes no sense. Use better grammar, would you?"

Inside of your being boy.

"That's no better."

You have to do it.

"Why?"

You know why.

"I sure as hell don't," he said, and he meant to protest more, but his mind defied him like a dog on the scent of memory, sniffing through the tangle of the past.

·→·→·←·←·

B oy. Child. There was a time when I was whole. The world was whole and I was bright inside it, moving through my days as if time itself were grace, it hurts to think of it, the distance between then and now, that and this, I shrink away from the memory the way I'd squint against the sun. But you said you wanted early so I'm going all the way back. Go on, take a look. Small boy in his freshly ironed school uniform, copying words from the blackboard and making faces across the aisle when the teacher isn't looking. Five years old, six, before my father died. I didn't know about death, or Marx, or the revolutionary dreaming to come, or the suffering of laborers, the government's ugly face. None of that had risen for me yet, and the world opened up before me like a gentle country lane. I walked the country lanes, rode my bike with the wind in my hair. How light I felt while riding, as if the wheels spinning against the earth could at any moment lift and soar and I'd be wheeling into the sky, toward that place where supposedly God sat in his big golden chair giving out love and commands. I wasn't sure what I'd do if I met God, whether I'd brake right at his feet and kiss them as my mamá would have wanted me to, or crash into his lap, or swerve off at the last minute into clouds and right back down to earth. So many good things on earth. The whip of air around me when I rode. The whip of wind through trees. The song of my little sister's laugh. The glow inside when I made my little sister laugh. The finding of ants and spiders by the creek. The smell of dirt after the rain. The heat of sun on skin. My father's face as he looked up from a newspaper to see me burst into a room. My mother's humming voice as she hung the laundry. My mother's stern voice in the morning, reminding me to work hard as she adjusted the lapels of my uniform before I set out for school. She expected the world of me. To her I was the world. To her I was the future of the world. Then seven years old. My father died. Everything changed. Now I was the man of the house, I had to think of other things, the things that added up to survival, which suddenly revealed themselves to me. You already know that story. Pesos. Markets. Bread. The vegetable garden my mother seeded to help feed us. Every plant in that garden mattered. Every stalk a belly-hope. Every root a tether to life. When you have your own vegetable garden, you unclasp, just a little, from the mercenary webbing of the human realm. You eat from what you grow with your hands. You cut out the middlemen and the bills and coins and go right to the source. You make your own sustenance, or, more accurately—because even that erases the main player— you tend the earth as the earth creates the sustenance you need.

That's how I started gardening: out of need. After need came love. Squatting in the dirt beside my mother, then without her as she cooked or cleaned, she had so much to do and the housework never stopped, so I took over the weeding and watering, seeding and pruning, watching and tending. The joy of dirt on my hands. Under my fingernails too far to clean. The good soreness of muscles. Squat down close. Dig deep, dig shallow, dig just right. Each plant has its own language, its own way of putting down roots. There is nothing like hearing them. Nothing like pushing your fingers into dirt.

Was this what you wanted? Are we going the right way?

You won't answer? Damn you.

I'll wait.

⟶⟶⟵⟵

I 'd like to touch on your personal style," the reporter said. "Your way of doing things."

The ex-president reached down and stroked Angelita's head. She was leaning against him now, at a slant; he felt the stump of her missing leg and the warmth of her underside along his thigh, burrowed close, closer than would have been possible if she'd had all her limbs. "All right. Please go ahead."

"You were never one for formal protocols." The reporter glanced down at her notes, as if she needed them, which, based on the past hour of conversation, she did not. "It's said that, during your whole presidency, you never once wore a tie."

"It's true." He shrugged. "I hate ties. They're uncomfortable, it's hard to breathe with your collar so tight, and in the summer? Who came up with the idea of wearing ties in the heat?" Colonists, he thought but did not say aloud. "Anyway, most people in this country, common

people, have never worn a suit and tie. Why shouldn't
they have a leader who reflects them?"

"And so, that's important to you? To look like the common people?"

"I am from the people. I still smell like the people."
He wasn't supposed to talk this way, about things like
his own scent. It was one of the many things his advisers had warned him about in the early years, and tried
to correct. Especially with foreign reporters, they said.
It doesn't translate, they won't understand, consider the
dignity of your office. But he'd grown comfortable with
this kind, spirited woman from Norway, and anyway, at
this point, what was the harm? What was there to lose?
He chided himself quickly: always a dangerous place to
start a thought. "This house I live in, it's closer to the
way the people live than any other presidential home has
been. That doesn't mean I speak for all the people. Of
course not. But I'm part of them, yes. We are an Us."

"An Us," she repeated slowly.

"Yes."

"At times, you've run into trouble, no? With these
choices? Once, when you attended a presidential inauguration in another country, the guards did not want to let
you in because they did not believe you could be a head
of state."

"I remember that day. I was wearing sandals. They couldn't understand the sandals. I couldn't understand how they expected me to wear socks on such a sweltering day." That hadn't been the only time, of course. Not everybody in his own country liked his style, not even in his own party, the third party, a young progressive party newly at the helm and built of so many leftist factions it was always a miracle they won as much as they did. So many visions of how to move forward. So much work to coalesce into motion. Once, at the presidential country estate, he'd gotten into trouble for hosting important people near a bathroom whose window let out onto a patio where he'd hung his and his wife's underwear to dry on the line. Mr. President, one of his advisers said, you cannot hang your laundry where your guests might see. Why not? he'd said, don't we all wear undies? But he'd had to let the staff take it down and commandeer the washing for the rest of that trip. Then there was the time he'd visited the King of Sweden and forgotten to formally present the gift he'd brought. He'd left it, wrapped, on the table, causing a bomb threat alert and filling the palace with soldiers. That hadn't been a matter of values, though, just absentmindedness and an overly freewheeling lack of decorum. He didn't like decorum and, yes, he had his reasons, but that day he'd learned something about the purpose it could serve.

"You drove your own car through the city," the reporter went on. "That little VW Beetle of yours—we've seen the pictures on the Norwegian news."

"Really? Well. Why not drive it? It's a nice little car, does the job, and I got tired of sitting in that presidential getup. Now, I know my bodyguards hated it when I got behind the wheel, I gave them a hell of a time, it was hard on them to have to constantly round me up, so I did ride in the presidential car sometimes, but never in the back the way presidential protocols usually have it, only in the front passenger seat."

"Why?"

"Because if someone was going to get shot I'd go down with the driver."

She blinked. "Is that serious?"

"Absolutely. What kind of man would I be if I just left them to it?"

"Isn't a president's life to be valued—well—more?"

"No."

"Not even for the sake of the country?"

"No."

She stared at him. It was impossible to read the expression on her face. Even the cameraman, hidden this whole time behind the lens, now craned his neck to openly study the ex-president. He thought of telling them it wasn't really such a big deal, as, after all, how much safer would he really be in the backseat or behind a flank of body-guards? Wouldn't the kinds of people who might want to kill him—the generals of his own country, the foreign CIA—always find a way? Once, during the presidency, there had been a knock on his door under cover of night, a military man, the visit brief and cryptic, the message crystal clear. *We could get you.* But so what? He'd faced death so long ago and watched so many of his comrades die that it had stayed part of the fabric of his days. But this seemed too much to say, so he simply shrugged and said, "Old guerrilla thinking."

"Ah." The reporter cocked her head. "Solidarity."

"If we don't have that, we're doomed."

The reporter seemed on the brink of saying something impulsive, something she hadn't planned, then stopped herself. "Along those lines, you declined not only to live in the Presidential Palace but also to have any staff to cook or clean for you."

"It's true. Why should being elected president mean you suddenly have a maid?"

"What about the new demands on your time?"

"Bah! Time to sweep is also time to think. The thing is, I may have become president but I was still a man. That's what people don't get about presidents. They should never be above the people, never be seen as better than anyone else. That's not reality. It's just an old colonial system that's been handed down from monarchist times, this royal treatment, and it shouldn't be that way. Presidents should not pretend they're kings." Fleetingly he thought of the news from the North, the man with the golden toilet who was too foolish (or too despicable, perhaps) to know the difference between presidents and kings, between crowns and places to shit. But that thought was tied to too many hauntings and he didn't want to follow them, not yet. He remembered, also, that Norway still had a king. Perhaps this wouldn't land so well with them and they'd take it the wrong way. Better to tread carefully. He softened his tone. "Look, I know other presidents see it differently, and fine, I'm not saying they're wrong. I have friends who are rich and enjoy being rich. It's been strange to see, but so what, good for them." There was more to it. There was always more to every story. He'd never had friends like that before rising in electoral politics. These were people who'd reached out to him as he rose to power, who wanted to help him, who had rich friends in other countries, access to an international network so potent it could not be seen, and they'd helped his presidency bring foreign investment in the door for businesses in his country and it had helped, had created jobs, and they were human beings too, these rich men, with their yachts and servants, watches that could feed a family of five for a year, they were capable of making heart connections and of helping the great project of lifting a people in a complex globalized world; after all, it wasn't every rich man who offered friendship to a president like him, it took the type who saw something in his vision and wanted to be part of it, and man, did they have ways to be part of it, they had leverage that he as president could never have accessed directly in ten lifetimes, because that was how international capitalism worked, and, no matter how he felt about international capitalism, no matter how much he'd dreamed of dismantling it outright in his youth, he had to accept that he lived within it and his country existed in it too, for better or for worse—that global web of power, those endless unseen threads—and he had to contend with it if he was to help his people have jobs, food, life. The future belongs to dreamers, he thought, but not to purists. "That's been normal for most of history, right? Wealthy people in charge? Most of my predecessors came from the prep schools, the country clubs. Not me. Not even close. That's not my world and I've gotten to know it better now, but I didn't come from it and I shouldn't have to pretend otherwise, shouldn't have to change who I am fundamentally in order to lead. That's not leadership at its best."

"It seems, to me, a completely different approach to power than what we usually see."

The wind rose and murmured in the trees. Angelita adjusted herself slightly but stayed close, her body relaxed against him.

"I'm not saying everybody has to live the way I do. It's just: it's who I am. It's the path that made sense to me and I was determined to live what was true to me, for there to be room for that in the world." He'd also hoped to inspire more people to follow his example, to volunteer most of their salaries to build houses for the poor, to join him in forging a new and more egalitarian economic path, a kind of at-will redistribution of wealth. It hadn't gone that way. He'd been surprised by this, by how, for all the press his donations had received, the people had not rallied to join him, had preferred to hold their money close. When he told his wife about his surprise, she'd only laughed.

Old man! For all your talk of pragmatism, look at you, an idealist after all! "A president who lives more or less normally, like the old anarchist he is."

The reporter smiled. "An old anarchist, as the head of state?"

He raised his eyebrows in mock alarm. "I'm afraid so."

"Is there a paradox here?"

He spread his palms open, as if to hold all their surroundings. "There's paradox everywhere."

"So where did this path come from, this way of living? Because you see, Mr. President"—she paused to tuck a strand behind her ear—"all over the world there are people who want to crack this code you've found or set in motion, to get inside the paradox, because, well, so many of us are hungry for new ways to understand power, and for new approaches to presidency but also leadership itself, the way we think about the shape of the world and who actually does the shaping of it and how and why, and in fact it seems as if we're at the cusp of an era when we'll need this new understanding more than ever, that we ignore these questions at our global peril, if you see what I mean, I'm not sure I'm expressing it correctly, I'm thinking aloud now, perhaps I'm not making sense?"

"You're making sense," the ex-president said, thinking, yes, I bet she gardens back in Oslo even if it's just in pots on the kitchen sill, I can see her plucking basil leaves for dinner as she chops and stirs and simmers the riot of thoughts in her mind.

"So what's the secret? How did you arrive here?"

He felt it again. The hovering at the edge. Temptation. To tell, to speak, to say things all the way through. She watched him, alert as a deer. He blinked, inhaled, waited for the urge to pass.

You've been quiet for a long time.

Y ou've been quiet for a long time. It was true, it had been forever, some elastic stretch of forever time during which sleep
had come and gone, food on a rope had come and gone,
meager light through the slats had come and gone and
still he'd kept his stubborn silence in the presence of the
frog. It had been like that blinking game he'd played with
classmates as a child and he'd always won it, always been
able to hold out until the other kid blinked no matter how
his eyes shouted and stung. "So have you."

You shouldn't have stopped.

"You shouldn't drive me nuts."

Hum-de-dum, where have you goooooone . . .

"I hate you."

Liar.

"All right, maybe that's not true—maybe I don't hate
you, you got me there. But still. You haven't said anything about what I told you." He felt the petulance rise

in him, sharp and childish, he knew, though he was too far gone to care. He'd held tight to this grudge for the whole long stretch of forever time in which they hadn't talked. "I did what you asked. Some of that, I'd never told anyone before."

Like?

"Like the part about biking all the way to God."

Oh! O-ho! The guerrilla fighter's deepest secret!

"Don't make fun of me."

Why not?

"I . . ."

What makes it such a secret? That it's a bike? Or that it's God?

"There is no God."

You say and say that.

"Well, it's true."

Then why is it mattering?

"Because, back then— Oh, hell, who cares, you wouldn't understand. What do you know about being human?"

What do you?

The question stabbed at him. He couldn't take it, no more stabbing. "Are you going to help me find your stupid Thing or not?"

So you haven't given up.

"Have you?"

The finding belongs to you.

"Great. Fucking wonderful."

Go on, go on.

"What's the point?"

We're closer than you think.

"You sure this time?"

There is no other time.

"How can that be?"

Where you were. In the dirt.

"The part about my hands in the dirt?"

Yes.

"You want me to tell you more about the dirt? Let's see, well, it was dirt—ah, it felt like poetry before, now it sounds stupid."

Why?

"I don't know. It's just—it's a small memory, no fireworks, nothing you'd put in anyone's biography, see what I mean?"

Small is everything. Everywhere.

"Huh."

It made you happy?

"The dirt? Of course."

Was it your first happy?

"No. I don't think so. But after my father died I needed

it, it was the first happiness after we lost him, because
after that my mother had to stretch every peso and the
days weren't easy, some of my classmates pitied me as
a fatherless boy and I hated that, their pity, even then
I knew we had less than some, more than others, and I
started learning the true meaning of class struggle from
those hungry days of—"

All well and good, but that's not it, go deeper.

"Deeper—where?"

To the first time you saw it.

"Saw what?"

The One Thing.

"That Holds Everything I Fucking Need."

Yes.

"Damn it, I've already told you, I don't know what it
is, I keep giving you my memories and you keep turning
them down."

Deeper is the way.

He searched inside, made an honest effort. "Sofía. No
one's touched me deeper than Sofía," he said, amazed to
realize, there, in that abysmal place, worlds away from
whatever abysmal place held her, that it was true. Would
he ever see her again? Would the bond still be there? It
seemed beyond possible, too much, shunt it far out of
mind.

No. That's good and fine. But it's faaaaaar away from the way in.

"So then what's the way in?" He was pleading now.

The first time.

"First time of what? First time I had sex? It wasn't so great, nothing to blare from the rooftops, I can tell you that right now, in fact it was embarrassing, I had a lot to learn but I caught up in the—"

No. Not that.

"Well, I'm at a loss. This was your crazy idea."

Deeper deeper.

"What am I looking for?"

The first time you saw it.

"Oh, for fuck's sake. Saw what? Wait, no please, don't say it—"

The One Thing you need.

—➤—◂—

W hat the hell, he thought, what the hell is this, I don't want to play this game anymore, time to get off the wheel and stop following this creature toward a nothing of his own invention, this ridiculous One Thing, who knows where he got the idea for it anyway, maybe nowhere, maybe he made the whole thing up and I followed him because I'm just plain dumb, because I had nothing else to do, as an escape, a lark, an unhinged game, a last-ditch lunge toward a maybe-life, a question mark hung inside a nightmare, a hope I couldn't believe in, or, worse, as a hope I pretended not to believe in but deep down couldn't help opening to, just a smidge, just a centimeter, damn hope, fucking hope, why did it have to invade him, stirring a secret part of him like the stick you poke around for the slightest ember in the ash. But what if there was nothing in the ash. What had he been thinking? Where was it all going? This frog had led him in circles and he was tired of being told he'd gone the wrong way, tired of traveling through memories, he was more than tired, he had nothing left, no steam, he wanted to stop, wanted it all to stop. And yet that wasn't true: he didn't want it all to stop. Not anymore, not quite. He was in something now, wasn't he? Even if he had no clue what the something was? And in any case, how would stopping be any better? Without this exasperating conversation he'd be back in the bleakness of before, prey to guards, ants, thirst, his own mind. The frog was his last tether, and he knew deep down—he now understood— that if the frog left before they finished he'd succumb to the horror, belong entirely to the hole. For this reason, he pushed on.

What else?

What else was there inside him?

"I don't know, man. I want to try, but I'm stuck."

Keep talking.

So he did. He rambled. He didn't know what he said. He talked until his mouth was drier than a desert stone. He paused when food descended on its rope, paused to collapse into sleep, but the frog didn't leave and he didn't stop even as the night stretched long around him. Hours passed, then days, and still the frog was listening, still he didn't know the way in or the way through. He meandered over memories, over time. He spoke of bread, school, his bicycle, wet mud after rain, skies turning dark, his sister singing, his sister pulling laundry off the line, the billowing of linens, the billowing of wind, the rattle of windows in the wind, the silent crawl of spiders, waking to a riot of birds, imagining himself flying off in a riot of birds, crying after his father died but only into his pillow because he was seven years old now, a big boy, a little man, nobody could ever hear, and nobody did find out he'd cried about his father until now, here, in the hole. He spoke of staring at pastries in the bakery window, ravenous for them, knowing they were out of reach. He spoke of the teacher's ruler smacking the back of his hand, the red swell of skin. He spoke of dirt. He kept circling back to dirt. What was it the frog had said about it? *This is where we need to go.* So he raised it up before him: dirt, in his hands, on his knees, beneath his feet, all around him. Weeding beside his mother, growing those flowers, tending the vegetables that kept them fed after they'd lost his father's income and had to make their way themselves, the proximity of hunger, the lack of hunger thanks to the slow reliability of the earth, the quiet alchemy that made it possible for a plant to grow. His mother taught him to tend to the vegetable garden, early on. An unfolding. A new power. A miracle to rival the Saints: sunlight turned into food. The apparition of zucchini. The benediction of flowers. The gospel of carrying bouquets to the open-air market, where he sold them to old women on their way to the cemetery to honor their dead, and the way he'd cut the stems when it came time to harvest, the particular slant that kept them fresh, there was an art to the cutting and he held it in reverence whether or not he'd have thought back then to use that word, he was proud to know that art, for it was an art, the way of flowers—and that's when he felt it. A slowing of time.

It's very near.

Swooping close into that corner of the past, which blooms open and reveals its bright and steady pulse.

Stay there.

The way.

Yes.

Of flowers.

Go all the way in.

"Here? This?"

Tell.

"There was a man who taught me about flowers. A neighbor. He grew them on his land, sold them, arranged them in his home." The memory swelled open, why so radiant? Where did it come from, that glow? "I worked for him when I was young and he showed me his trade."

Tell more. Tell deep.

"About my flower-teacher?"

Yes.

"That's where it is? The mystery thing we're looking for?"

Don't you know?

"You're the one who—"

Are you really such an idiot?

"All right, all right."

All the way in.

And so he tried.

⟶⟶⟵⟵

Once upon a time there was a boy who learned the way of flowers. It was me. I was about eleven years old when I started helping out on Mr. Takata's land. By then, I'd been with the bakery for a good while, and the owner was nice enough but didn't really need me anymore, he had his nephews behind the counter now, and he seemed relieved I had another place to go. Mr. Takata's land was a three-minute walk from our home, wide and open, with row upon row of flowers growing bright into the air, and my job was to water them, tend them, and, later, once I'd proven myself, cut and harvest them, which is a skill, you know, more subtle than you'd think. He knew all about it, Mr. Takata, he knew the way of flowers. There was no one like him. He died a few years ago, when I was at the prison in the city, you know, the one I escaped from; Mamá told me on one of her visits and it gutted me not to be able to go to the funeral. Mr. Takata. When I was eleven, Mamá told

me I was lucky he'd taken me on, that I should always
be respectful and make myself as useful as I could. I
wanted to be useful. I wanted to learn. I can see them
now, those blooms, vibrant and fragile at the same time,
and my hands came to love them, to long for their petals
and stems. I didn't know yet that this work would change
my life. That I'd come to grow my own flowers on our
back patio. That I'd sell blossoms on the bus to school,
sell blossoms for a living, become a florist who secretly
organized for the revolution or a revolutionary who prac-
ticed floristry between secret meetings. That flowers and
revolution would become my twin tasks—and you know
what, now that I really think about it, I wonder whether
any of that would have happened without Mr. Takata,
whether flowers would have commanded such a space in
my life and soul.

Because his love was palpable, you see. Love and other
elements I never put into words back then but you could
feel it in the way he handled his plants, a way I'd never
seen. Mr. Takata had arrived only a few years before
from Japan with his wife, Mrs. Takata, and he'd bought
this land soon after, tilled it, started a new life. He was
sparing in his speech, careful with his words, which were
new to him, by which I mean our language was new to
him and came out inflected with the sounds of his native

tongue, for which the neighborhood children mocked him behind his back, exaggerating his accent and pulling their eyes at the edges as they passed the gate to his land, but Mamá said I was never to do this and so I never joined in although—I don't want to say this part but, hell, you said go all the way so here I go—I never stopped the neighbor kids either, nor the grown-ups who watched them do it and laughed along. I never stood up for my boss who was my flower-teacher too. The shame of it. Stabs me now.

But am I rambling?

Am I veering too far?

How do I get to the One Thing?

You're not going to tell me, are you?

Be silent, then, see if I care. Damn it. All right. Mr. Takata was a master. That's what none of the neighbor kids would ever see. He spoke the language of flowers and he taught it to me. There we are on the land, bent over carnations, side by side, cutting stems with just the right diagonal line. Sharp shears he'd brought over from Japan, with looped handles, you'd never find anything like that in our country, it took a while before he let me use them but eventually he did. One of the few things I brought with me, he once said. But wait. Hold on. When he said that: it wasn't in the fields, we were inside his house. In the living room. It was the same size as my family's living room, but it felt much more spacious, because there were so few things in it, each object artfully placed rather than cluttering a corner in a throng. I'd never seen a living room like that before. Where other living rooms chattered with color and objects, this one seemed, I don't know how to put it—not quiet, no, because the opposite of raucousness is not quiet. It's something else. Room for each voice, each shape and thing, to vibrate on its own terms. It had taken months for Mr. Takata to invite me inside. I'd worked hard in those months and he'd relaxed with me. His wife offered me tea, in Japanese, repeated in Spanish by Mr. Takata, and when I nodded they spoke to each other for a few moments in Japanese, a sound like nothing I'd ever heard before and I couldn't distinguish separate words in the river of their speech. It flowed over pebbles of meaning, smoothing them, or so it seemed at least in my ears. As they talked, it occurred to me that maybe Mr. Takata wasn't always as taciturn as I'd seen him to be, as he'd been with me or with our neighbors, that there were other sides of him that existed at home, that existed in Japanese, and I was just now getting a glimpse of those sides, the smallest peek but enough to amaze me. Mrs. Takata went to the kitchen and returned a little later with a cup of tea. She placed it before me.

Her face was worn, kind. The tea was a strange flavor, alarming, but I didn't dare say a word. I drank the tea and smiled at Mrs. Takata, who looked at me for a long moment—she didn't speak my language, I realized, it was the first time I'd met eyes with someone whose lexicon was altogether different from my own; I said thank you and we smiled at each other, almost shyly, and then she bowed slightly and retreated to the kitchen. Mr. Takata was arranging flowers in a vase, three stalks, with a tender precision that made me think of the Renaissance painters we'd learned about in school, how every brushstroke mattered and gave something to the whole. As always I was mesmerized by his hands, their power, their steadiness, the bright hum they drew out of blooms. One of the few things we brought, Mr. Takata said, those shears. We could only bring small things. And then he talked. More than he ever had to me before. I sat and listened, stunned, my hands warmed by the cup of tea. He used to live in a city. They'd fled it, bombs were coming, it was the War, they'd left with very few things, he was a doctor back then—I hadn't known this, had not imagined—but had always tended flowers, out of love, he said, gingerly prolonging the word *amor;* in Japan, he added, the tending of flowers was revered. There was a word for it in

Japanese whose roots came from the word for flowers and the word for making things alive. It gave him a feeling he wasn't sure how to describe in Spanish, he said, but a feeling that was important, to make things alive. Now his city was destroyed, many people had died—and as a boy I didn't know yet how to see under the surface of that simple statement, who might have been implied and grieved in that small phrase *many people,* parents, sisters, brothers, neighbors, friends—and now in this new land he could not do the work he did before, but, he said, hands still on the flowers, eyes meeting mine, eyes lingering, he could grow things.

Grow things.

What's happening, I can't think.

Why is this wetness on my face? Am I weeping? I thought I'd lost my tear ducts in the torture rooms, I really did, what is this, what are you doing to me. Mr. Takata. He showed me. All the sorrow, all the grief, it was right there in his eyes but I couldn't take it in, an intensity I saw but could not recognize, I was a boy, what did I know, I'd lost my father, sure, couldn't afford the fancy pastries, but so what, my mother still adored me and my country was still whole— I can't. No. That can't be where you—

My country was still whole and

When a country breaks what else can
Mr. Takata, Mr. Takata, can you—
Do I
Can you see me?
In this hole?
Reaching out to you?

⟶⟶⟵⟵

T he hole expanded, glowed, fell open, swung. In
poured the world. In glided Mr. Takata's hands.
They were just as he remembered, steady, long-
fingered, skilled and precise, only they grew larger by the
second, growing as large as this hole and maybe even large
enough to hold the pain, could that be possible? Could
any hands in the universe hold the pain? Loss of country,
of home, of safety, of lives, of the world as you knew it
before? He exposed his soul to these hands. They grew
to the size of a house, enormous hands, refugee hands,
sorrow stored in bones that were not broken, that cupped
toward each other as if ready to hold water, a petal, a sac-
rament. Or him. Could they hold him. Where was the
frog. In the corner, there. Silent. Witness. And where was
his own voice. He couldn't speak, his throat ached with
a fullness out of which no sound could come, and so he
did the only thing left to do: he gave himself over to the
hands. Climbed into them. They formed a nest around

him, a gentle boat, a blossom. He curled into the hands like a human seed. Let this be real, he thought. Let me be tended. Let me stay here in these hands that have known nation-grief as well as petals in the thousands, the earth's most flagrant speech, let me stay here forever, though even then he understood that forever was not to be, for however broken he might be after four years of prison, however starved and blistered and flooded with despair, however sure he'd been that everything was over for his country and his life—that his nation was destroyed, that the world as he knew it was destroyed—he now saw, in a sharp flash, as he lay in Mr. Takata's cupped enormous palms, that despite all his fears and secret hopes he had not fully lost his mind.

Nor his hands.

Nor a chance, however slight, of one day being free.

And if he got that chance he now saw that he had to take it, had to stand up and keep on, carry forward what was given, grow things, make things alive.

─➤─◄─

S o," the reporter said, leaning back into her chair, "are we ready to talk about the North?"

In the distance, a bird cawed into the warm spring air. The afternoon light was starting to grow languorous, rich and heavy in its journey toward the dark.

"No," the ex-president said.

"No?"

He stayed deadpan. "We'll never be ready."

"Ah." She scanned his face, laughed for a moment, fell serious. "You're right. Nothing could prepare us for this moment."

Nothing and everything, he thought but did not say.

"Norway is reeling. Many people were stunned. Over what it means for the future, but also, how it could happen. How could anyone vote for such a man?"

It seemed to be not an interview question, but a rhetorical one. He felt her mask slipping, felt the boundaries of one-way inquiry blurring toward the realm of conversation, a comfortable realm for him, akin to home. "Sometimes people vote their fears, or vote for the story the candidate tells them that they want to believe is true."

"But *that* story—the things he's said—it's so ugly. Bigoted. Dangerous."

"Yes, well." It was so new—not the ugliness, which was as old as recorded history, and certainly as old as recorded history in the Americas, but, rather, this change in the global order. He'd only just begun to shape words around his thoughts; they tossed and whirled inside him, but he did not have the luxury to wait until his thoughts were crystalline, because he was a former president and therefore was expected to have solace, warnings, insights at the ready. And, anyway, crystalline might never come; you might never be absolutely sure of what the hell was going on, so better not to wait around holding your tongue. "We are in danger."

She seemed startled by the bluntness. "Are we?"

"Yes." He was almost amused; it was such an obvious statement—but of course, it might sound particularly ominous coming from him, the so-called beacon of hope. "Of course." Not that the danger was new, either, more of a swelling of dangers extant in the world, and it was not the first time that a country entered the terrible reality of an incompetent would-be despot with no moral compass at the wheel, nor would it be the last, and it wasn't even the first time that a country with outsize power ceded its helm to a despot to the severe detriment of the rest of the world, but that had never gone well on a global scale and he doubted those words would reassure her. He was surprised to see that inside himself, the impulse to reassure.

"I—" She seemed to hover at the edge of a thought, undecided. "I am afraid," she finally said. "More than ever."

There were a thousand things he could have said, but he sensed it was not his turn, that there was more at the tip of her tongue and he should wait for her to go on. *Women have just as much to say as men,* Sofía often said. *But we keep getting interrupted.* The School of Sofía, he liked to call it, his own private university, which tickled them both as he'd never completed any higher degree, and I don't need to, he'd tell her, you and life are the only professors I need. That was in the good moments, of course, not the ones where Sofía pointed out that he'd talked over a woman in a meeting, that he had to learn to back up and let women speak. Years ago that kind of observation on her part would drive him into days of grumpiness and self-pity, for hadn't he always been welcoming of women in leadership? Didn't he respect her more than he respected anyone? How could she accuse him of the thing he'd seen other men do, the way they broke in when women were talking, pompously, in love with the sound of their own voices, he wasn't pompous like that, didn't she know? Those men who cut her off in the halls of Congress, he mocked them with her, he wasn't anything like them, how could she—? Years, it took, for him to grudgingly accept that it wasn't only the pompous ones, that it could be the good ones too, that she was teaching him something he'd failed to learn on his own. Something that wasn't only about etiquette and how to be more balanced in conversations, but about something deeper, too, how to shape liberation so that it includes everyone, how to see the places where you assumed you'd included everyone but hadn't, how to widen the channels, push the revolution to live up to its own dreams. Leave no one out. Not women, not Black people, not gays or transgender people or indigenous people or immigrants or refugees. In the old days, he'd considered their revolution the widest vision there could be. What a surprise to hear that questioned in recent years. Younger activists were quick to critique the past. It irked him, but he'd also learned some things. Even now he didn't always get it right, but at least he understood a little more than he did before and was more willing to be humbled, to be wrong, to try again. *You love to talk,* Sofía said to him once, late at night, *there's nothing wrong with that, in fact we all want your talk, we need it. But you have to listen, too.* And he'd replied, I don't want to be like them, the pompous ones. And she gave him a look of amusement and said, *then don't be.* Now he, a former president who loved to talk, subject of the interview, used his School of Sofía training to keep his mouth closed and wait.

A bird cawed over their heads as it soared away.

The reporter opened her mouth, closed it. Opened it again. "I want to be optimistic, I truly do. But I'm at war with myself. There's so much to worry about, starting with the safety of Muslims, immigrants, people of color in that country. Then there's the potential catastrophic impact on the rest of the world. Look at climate change: I can't imagine how we'll be moving forward now on international accords, how we're going to meet the enormous challenge facing the planet. Not to mention what we'd face if there were some kind of international emergency on his watch."

"Anything could happen."

"Yes."

"And, of course, climate change *is* an international emergency," he said. "The greatest one we'll face, no matter what else shows up."

"Yes, yes," she said, reflexively, almost dutifully, with

that slight glaze over her voice he'd grown accustomed
to hearing in response to the climate crisis. People didn't
know they were doing it. A human response to the gar-
gantuan. She paused, as if deliberating whether to further
pursue the subject, and he braced himself, preparing to
calibrate his answers so she wouldn't hear the full depth
of his pain at what was coming for his country, for all
countries, the harm already caused among the most
vulnerable because that was always where harm began,
how to sound the alarm without sounding alarmist,
how to foment calm and wake people up to the severity
all at once, for the truth was that people didn't want to
hear it, didn't want to think the systems they relied on
were about to be strained in unprecedented ways, that
the systems were fragile, that the flaws in the systems
could widen exponentially under pressure, that the harm
would be beyond what any human mind could conceive,
nobody wanted to hear that shit from a so-called beacon
of hope, he didn't want to hear it either but he'd seen it,
listened to the briefings, read the reports, felt it all roil-
ing through his dreams. Often he woke in a sweat that
seemed composed of furious storms, the storms inside his
dreaming, which flooded towns and swept up lives and
delivered him wet and short of breath into his own bed,
limbs on fire, still haunted by the clamor of the drowned.

And yet it would not do to give the dreams a voice, only the urgency behind them. How to tell this, how to shape it into words—but the reporter barreled on. "And then there's the question of how this could embolden a global rise of the far right. In Norway, we never really wanted to believe it was there, our own ugly right wing, or that it had any strength or connection to the core of who we are as a culture, until the mass shooting five years ago. I'm sure you recall it."

He did. He'd sat in his presidential office, listening to an aide read the brief aloud: a lone-wolf gunman, in Norway, not a Muslim as had initially been assumed but a white supremacist, a bomb, an automatic weapon, a summer camp with children of leftist party leaders, blood, blood, blood, children punished for the sins of their fathers and the sin was what, letting in immigrants, letting in brown people, refusing to hate. He'd stared across the room as the aide kept talking and the words poured over him in pure undecoded sound and for a few moments he was no longer at his desk on the American continent but on a Norwegian island where he filled a river of blood with his own river of tears, and the great temptation was to fall into that river and forget everything, give up, glide forever away. But no. He was in his office. He was being briefed. His eyes were dry. There was work to do. He launched forward into his day, pushing the river down to the subterranean layers of his mind, from which it rose up now to fill him with fresh grief as well as horror, because there would be more of that now, after this election in the North. There would be more, in the country where the man had been elected, without a doubt, and also beyond it, for speech was global now and spilled over national borders in the blink of an eye. *Blood, blood, blood,* he could have said but did not say to the reporter. He wasn't sure she would believe him if he tried to speak the horror, the violence to come; people couldn't always see what they couldn't bear to imagine, and the fewer bleak times you've lived through, the less you see them coming. He shifted the channel of his thoughts. "Of course. A terrible thing."

"It broke us. Broke us open. A rise in incidents like that—" She stopped, inhaled sharply, as if air were scarce.

—is probable, he thought, as an end to her sentence. But instead, he said gently, "I also remember the outpouring of solidarity in Oslo. Flowers. Crowds. Signs bearing beautiful messages."

She nodded. "I took my son to the vigils. He was only four then, and frightened, but we had to go, I had to show him and he already knew. His cousin—my nephew, he was at that camp—"

Her face broke open, sound caught in her throat.

"I am so sorry," the ex-president said, only because he lacked any other words. Bleak times. He'd made an assumption about her First-World life. But what did he know about what she carried inside? He was not so much surprised as he was struck by how impossible it was to ever gauge how a person existed in their skin, the way the world pressed down on them, the exact shape and weight of the pressing. The dead nephew arose, a phantom, a slip of light, haunting the garden with his beauty.

"I'm the one who's sorry," the reporter said, not moving to wipe the tears from her face. "I've strayed off topic."

The ex-president wanted to hear more about the nephew, about her son, and especially about the vigil, how they'd done it, found their way through. How long they'd walked the streets, whether her son had carried flowers to an altar or himself been carried in his mother's arms, or both, a flower in the hands of a boy in the arms of his mother, a boy still young enough for those arms to be the world. Whether they'd held silence, or sung one of the songs of peace that had filled the vigils. The colors of their flowers. Flowers, flowers, their colors weaving a dirge. "You're not off topic at all," he said. "In fact, it's possible this is the only topic that exists."

She gazed at him in silence, hungry for something from him, from this man she'd called Mr. President, even though the time in office was done, such a strange convention, referring to an ex-president as if he still inhabited the name. He waited, allowing her space, and suddenly he wondered how many more interviews there would be before death came to take him, how many more afternoons like this one, and then it struck him that there would never be another afternoon exactly like this one ever again. The thought filled him with a feeling between sadness and awe. She was still staring at him and for a terrible moment he had no idea what to do, what to say, what to offer her, for there was nothing that could erase the pain and well he knew it, so he sat there and followed his instinct and let her look at him, let himself be seen.

In the distance, a car moaned down the road. Finally, she dried her face with careful hands. When she spoke again, her tone was steady, her face composed. The moment had passed. "I was so struck by your reaction when you first heard the election results, last week."

"You read about it?"

She nodded. "I've seen the footage."

"I was in Italy, walking out of my hotel in the early morning, when a cluster of journalists approached me."

"Yes, and they gave you the news and asked for comment." Now she looked almost amused. "Perhaps you hadn't planned any remarks?"

"I didn't have time. I learned the news right then and there. And anyway, you know how I am." He waved a hand through the air. "I say the first thing that springs to my head. I'm not a perfect man but I'm an honest one. I believe people should say what they really think."

"Even in politics?"

"Especially in politics. I mean, what is politics?"

"You tell me."

"It's the struggle to give all people joy and freedom."

She arched an eyebrow. "Nothing else?"

There was so much more he could say, a thousand words at the tip of his tongue, teeming with the urge to be heard, for what had all these years been if not a foray into that very question and how many raucous answers had he found, more than he could possibly sort out in a single lifetime. Better to hew to the inner compass he'd returned to over and over and that had not yet led him astray. "Nothing."

All this time, as the future president had lain in the nest of Mr. Takata's hands, the frog had stayed quiet. Watching without a word.

The man reached out and picked up the small, cool body. It was the first time they'd ever touched and the frog made a sound like a guttural sigh as he relaxed into the man's hands.

He held the frog against his chest, not far from the beating of his own heart. A frog cradled in the hands of a man in turn cradled by giant hands.

Warmth spread through him, the warmth of an embrace, different from the embrace of Sofía, of past lovers, of his mother, whom he pushed out of mind as he'd always done these past four years so as to protect her from this bleak place but no, stop, wait, said a voice inside him, let your mother breathe inside your mind, you damn coward, give her that at least, and so he did, he let his mother in, let her rise inside his consciousness, Mamá, Mamá, can you feel me, can you hear me, do you know that your boy is still alive, I am sorry, Mamá, for the pain, the worry, whatever you've suffered. To these brutal bastards I will never apologize for anything but I owe the world to you. Whether or not his mother would ever hear his thoughts he could not say. He rocked the frog against his chest, cupped him gently, his first embrace in four years. In all that time he'd known either no touch or rough touch, the guards' touch, though he only realized it now that he was in contact with another living being. The warmth kept spreading through him, made his fingers tingle, woke his skin, surged blood into his sex, what was that, could it be, yes, holy hell, he thought, I've got an erection, not rock-solid, nothing to brag about but that's a boner all right, and this embarrassed him more than he'd ever dare say, here was a tale to keep buried for the ages, no one could know it happened until the end of time, a hard-on from holding a frog, who ever heard of such a thing, and yet— why not admit it?—the humiliation was shot through with relief at what his cock could do, he hadn't gotten truly hard since freedom, since before the Machine, at least his body was still capable of it, the electric nodes on his genitals hadn't shocked all that out of him forever after all, good to know, might come in handy if he ever got out of this godforsaken place and there, he thought, is an optimistic thought at last, well look at that, it flashed quickly past but he relished it all the same, an optimistic thought in a place like this was to be savored, a flash of humor was better than gold, the frog was cool in his cupped hand and against his chest, the sweet burden of him, the gladness, he hadn't touched anyone or been touched in months and how much of the madness could he have staved off with just a little touch of the right kind? The frog was breathing, he was breathing, their rhythms interlaced though they were not the same. Together they formed a jagged and oddly perfect song.

He fell asleep this way, with the frog against his chest, still enfolded in Mr. Takata's enormous hands. He dreamed of Sofía in a blue dress, laughing. She was at an urban beach, at the river's edge, he knew the one because he could see the city's Ferris wheel in the background, the one with the sweeping view of downtown and the endless stretch of river, it loomed behind her, turning, turning, its carriages empty—where had the people gone? Sofía, he called out to her. Sofía. The river stabbed with light. She turned to face him and her mouth moved as if to speak but there was no sound.

When he woke up, there were no giant hands and the frog was gone.

The hole was as it had been before.

The man waited for his friend for a long time. A day, two days, twenty. But that was it. There was no more. He never saw the frog again.

→>–<←

Some weeks later, he was removed from the hole and
taken to a solitary cell aboveground for an elastic
and uncertain amount of time, then to another,
and another. Things changed and stayed the same. Each
time he was moved, blindfolded in the back of a military
truck, he was able to confirm that his two brothers from
the struggle, his comrades, were still close by, had been
in the same place with him and would be in the next place
too, two solitaries alongside his own. Who knew what
epic battles played out in each of their cells. Sometimes,
in some of the places, he could hear the passing of guards
more frequently and even make out the distant groans of
his comrades or of other unknown prisoners, all of which
reminded him of the existence of humans, the ongoing
business of humanity, which was a tether to the world,
however sordid its expression might be.

The floors were mostly concrete, cold to sleep on, very
few dirt floors anymore. There were ants sometimes,

and spiders, but now they rarely screamed, and never spoke. And there were no frogs. He listened for them, waited, sometimes felt a jolt of hope at movement in dark corners, but no frogs came; of course, that it should be the particular frog he'd come to know was impossible, he could never have followed military trucks across the countryside and found his way into a far-flung cell, how could it even cross his mind, what was he thinking, he had no good reason whatsoever to keep hunting in the shadows for a creature whose company he craved.

Sometimes, he called up his memories of their conversations. Every shred of their exchange felt precious now, even the irritation, the circling, the barbs. All of it was part of something larger, like phrases from a treasured book, and with nothing to read but his own mind he let their spoken words live in him like text, fanned them out like petals, brash, daring their color into the world.

It was not always enough. He was not healed. It was not possible to be healed. The only possible miracle was to remain alive. Sanity was still a tenuous cord; he held on to it sporadically, let it go and fell, fought against the swarming nightmares until he rose again on whatever rope he could find, a thought, a word, a sound.

Four more years passed.

He was still alive.

THE PRESIDENT AND THE FROG

The storm began to lift when he was finally granted books.

He was also granted visits from his mother. She brought him her face, alive with love and the most ferocious determination to help him survive. He looked for reproach or blame in her eyes, in her body language—it was her right—but couldn't find it. She wasn't allowed to touch him but the sight of her was enough, almost too much to bear. She brought scraps of news, about his sister, who was happily married though she'd never been able to have children; about his sister's husband, who'd come over recently and quietly without being asked repaired a fence; about the neighbors' grandchildren, springing tall. She also brought him all the books she could. The authorities permitted only science books, anything else was still too dangerous, any books containing humans or human-born ideas could be subversive and therefore were strictly forbidden.

He read every word the way a starved dog gnaws at a bone. Agronomy. Biology. The span of galaxies through outer space. The molecular structure of water, the cellular structure of everything you could call alive. Every sentence was alive. Every page a balm for his eyes. His mind leapt to meet the consciousness imprinted in those texts, drew on sentences as rivers that could carry him afloat. The authorities could not have guessed that, for all they'd tried to avoid any tomes of human thought, they'd given him the closest thing to holy books for a man like him. No God but nature. No God but the collective Us. He looked for the collective Us in those pages, sought oracular hints for human mysteries. What are we, he thought ferociously, what are we? In the crush of all this glory—mitochondria and magma and protons and, holy shit, seeds—where do we find ourselves? One answer that kept rising: we were not built to be alone. We don't exist in a vacuum. Ecology: the most subversive subject of them all. The ultimate secret socialist tract. We were made to connect and to give a fucking crap about each other—it's right there in the science. Whether it's the spread of a disease, the balance of a food chain, or ripples in the weather, everything this one does affects that one, and so forth and so forth on end. We're bound to each other's fates by invisible threads whether we choose to admit it or not, and we deny those connections at our peril. Sure, we're mammals, so we're built for closeness, but it's not just true for us, it's true down to the least social organisms, which are still fed by what surrounds them, sustained by it, and nourish it in turn, bugs, plants, fungi; it's everywhere; even stars forge their own gravity to keep planets in orbit through the cold and lonely dark.

He still thought often about the frog, about the One Thing, Mr. Takata's giant hands. He imagined them sometimes, those hands, back around him, and though they never again returned with the same visceral radiance, the version he managed to call up was enough to calm his body, allow him to endure. Alone he was still part of a vast lineage of loss and suffering, reaching back in time through all the horrors of before—suffering and, sometimes, survival. In all that time, in all the days that followed the conversations with the frog, before the books and after them, no matter how dull or brutal or cold or hot his days became, no matter how fear or sorrow stabbed him or how grief for his nation raked its claws through his soul, he never again yielded to the temptation to die. Not once. He knew, from then on, that he wanted to live, and that, although he could not know whether he'd ever be free again, he'd keep on living for as long as the bastards let him, behind bars or beyond them; whatever life served up to him, he'd keep on breathing and fighting and loving—for what else could you call it, this will to breathe and fight—with everything he had.

And, he thought to himself, fiercely, on his better days, which flashed sporadically over the years, if I ever get out, if I ever have another day of freedom, I will grow things—I'll plant in every scrap of dirt I can, damn right

I will, I'll find some land to call my own and fill it with seeds and tend them like motherfucking crazy, I'll grow stems and leaves and fruits and flowers to shine up at the open sky, that same sky I miss so much I'd give my right arm to see it, I'll reach up to the sky with my hands and with the things I grow, zucchini, tomatoes, beets, chard, carrots, oregano, mint, parsley, carnations, roses, irises, lilies, and daisies goddamn, daisies for kilometers on end.

＊

᠁

B ack to that moment with the press," the reporter
said. "When you learned the news about the U.S.
election results. You said, 'I have one word for
you'—"

The former president joined in, and they spoke it
together: "¡Socorro!"

Socorro. Help. SOS. Save Our Souls. An exclamation
for the drowning.

They shared a smile at the sound of their merged voices.

"That's right," she said. "You said, 'socorro.' And then
you kept on walking."

"I did."

"Could you elaborate?"

He wasn't sure he could elaborate. He opened his mouth
to try, thinking, ¡Socorro!, why indeed? It was true, what
he'd told her a moment earlier, that he'd said the first
thing to spring to mind. He'd gotten up that morning in
his hotel room without a newspaper, without a laptop,

and the reporters had been waiting in the lobby. They'd caught him in a moment of pure reaction. After he said it, they'd shuffled and glanced around at each other, as if for permission to laugh, and they did laugh, though nervously, what to do, what did this ex-president mean, it was a joke, was it, wasn't it, though it went without saying that the matter could not be more serious—and yes, it had been a joke but also deadly real. Help! Help! What else to say? But who was going to answer that plea? Who would fly down to save them? Superman? Batman? Those superheroes from old imported comic books in which the crowds looked up to the sky and called socorro? There was no such thing as socorro. There was never any socorro in this world. You could fall into a hole and nobody would come for you as you starved and stared endlessly into the dark. You could be attacked by forces of power with nowhere to run. The world as you knew it could break or collapse or go up in flames and no one would fly down from the sky on cue to save it, there was no cure, no escape, no refuge, and then he heard Sofía's voice in his ears from years ago, *the only refuge left is what we give each other,* and as he breathed the garden air that bound him to the reporter and the cameraman and the trees and the cultivated green he thought, well, perhaps, why not, there is no socorro unless you count the socorro we can make ourselves, however we shape it, whatever it costs, we make it for ourselves and for each other and that's all there is, for a person, for a country, for a world; the superhero doesn't exist and at the same time the superhero is you, plain you, weird you, broken you, standing in the crowd as it stares at the sky for an answer. The only socorro. It's nowhere and everywhere. It comes from no one and from anyone, and it's all we have.

He was startled to realize he'd been talking. What had he said? How much of his thoughts had left his mouth? The reporter was watching him closely, keenly absorbing each word.

"Thank you so much for that," she said. "What an answer."

He resisted the urge to ask *thank you for what? what did I say?* It was too late, after all, to unsay it. So instead, he raised his eyebrows and smiled.

"I could keep listening to you for days, and I have a thousand more questions, but we've already taken so much of your time. I believe we are finished."

So soon? the ex-president thought, though it had been almost two hours, judging by the shifting light. He felt an odd twinge in his chest. "If you're sure."

But the cameraman had already started loosening the camera from its tripod.

The reporter nodded. "We are so grateful."

They looked at each other in a silence in which he tee-tered on the brink of saying almost anything, of saying too much. He felt as though he'd known this woman for years. As if he wouldn't be surprised to see her in his gar-den every breezy afternoon. As if he'd miss her terribly if she didn't appear. It seemed she might be thinking some-thing similar, but how could he know? They held each other's gaze for what seemed like a long time. Then she stood. The cameraman had finished packing his equip-ment. Time to go.

The ex-president rose, thinking, get ahold of yourself, old man. He gestured toward the house. "After you."

The reporter walked just ahead of him, and look at that, he hadn't said a word about the frog, he'd kept that shell closed the whole time, but it had pulsed below the surface of their conversation and now some deep-sea part of him was disappointed, unfinished, still hungry to tell after all these years during which the oyster had stayed shut on the ocean floor, and for an instant he imagined himself calling to her like a little boy who's had a big adventure or skinned his knee and is burning to give someone the story, someone who could listen, look, look, see how the skin broke, you'll never guess how it happened, I can't believe it myself, and wait until you hear what it took for me to pick myself up from the ground, wait till you hear what was waiting for me once I got up, more adventure, you won't believe it but here's proof, look at the dirt under my fingernails, look at how it's caked right in my wound, who knows, it might lodge in there forever and I'll have a bit of earth inside my skin, can you see, can you feel, can you imagine. But no. She was going and he was not a little boy, the interview was done. The reporter gave him a kiss on the cheek at the front door, as was the custom in this country, she'd read about their customs in some guidebook or more likely on the Internet, where so many customs come alive these days, and it seemed she'd gotten past the initial handshake stage.

"Thank you again," she said, then paused as if on the verge of saying one more thing.

He wanted to tell her to come back in. He wanted to give her something but couldn't begin to imagine what. It was certainly true that she could have been his grand-child, if, that is, he'd ever had children, could maybe even be his great-grandchild if he'd gotten started early on; that was the one great regret of his life, not having children, but he and his wife had spent their fertile years on the revolution and in holes. Was it some sort of grand-paternal instinct, this sudden wash of tenderness? He had nothing in his hands, nothing to give her except the words and time he'd already passed along.

So he only smiled at her.

She smiled back, and then she turned away and walked toward the van that would take her to the rest of her life.

Dust flared on the dirt road as they drove away.

He took a deep breath. Twilight had started to gather its skirts. Sofía wouldn't be home for a few more hours. Back inside, he found Angelita curled up in his regular chair by the woodstove, as if to say, coming or what? But he didn't want to stay inside. Not yet. He picked up the yerba mate and thermos he'd brewed when the crew arrived, and returned to the garden, heading down the path this time, realizing he'd never taken the reporters around the curve to see the vegetables and the flowers, damn it, they were going to go at the end but it was too late now. Though not for him. There they were. His zucchini. Tomatoes. Beets. Chard. Beyond them rose the flowers, the sight of which unlatched something inside him, swung it open. Maybe next time a reporter asked him why he'd lived so humbly he'd reply that it wasn't humility at all, but survival, and a form of surrender to a basic natural law. Tend the earth and let it tend you back.

He pulled a stool close to the tangle of tomato plants,

and sat. A few years ago he would have squatted right down in the dirt, but that was too hard for him now. He felt an ache in his chest, though he didn't know why. Or perhaps he did. He turned his attention to the tomatoes, which were riotous with small green fruit, promising an excellent harvest. This summer, he'd make many jars of tomato preserves, even more than last year, perhaps forty. Enough to last all year round. Last year, he'd been exhausted by the canning, but even old age couldn't stop him from doing it again this year. They enjoyed them all year long, those tomato preserves, especially on Sofía's homemade pizzas, which always reminded him of the first meal they ever cooked in this house, when they'd first bought the land, to celebrate the miracle of home. They'd only been out of prison for a year; they'd found each other as soon as they got out and, after thirteen years of solitary confinement dreaming of Sofía, he'd tried to prepare himself for disappointment. Years had passed. They'd both been shattered. She might be distant, she might want nothing to do with a man who reminded her of the old days, she might want nothing to do with a man at all and who would blame her. But the second he saw her again, he knew. They could still speak to each other without speaking, and they communicated everything, right then and there, in silence, how the longing had stayed with them, a source of desperately needed warmth. They would brave the world together from now on. A year later, they bought the land with its ramshackle little house and she made pizza from scratch on their first night there. He'd watched her spoon tomato sauce onto fresh dough in the dim light and it seemed the most beautiful possibility on earth. I'm going to grow tomatoes here, he told her. To which she replied, without looking up, we're going to grow everything here, everything we can. Now, decades later, Sofía still had steam in her; she'd been the first First Lady in the history of her country to simultaneously serve as congresswoman, a job she still had now, which was why she was out this evening and wouldn't be home till well after dark. *Long meeting tonight,* she'd said this morning as she kissed him goodbye on the lips. In her spry mid-seventies, her vitality seemed unstoppable. He'd stay up for her, he thought, and when she arrived he'd heat the lentil stew and boil water for yerba mate, ask about her day, they'd swap stories as the night grew long.

For now, nothing to do but sit here in the garden, listen to the gathering dark, and wait.

He poured himself a yerba mate, and drank. He stared at the plants. He stared at his hands. The wrinkles still shocked him, though wrinkled hands could still be skilled ones, as he'd learned in childhood as he watched the hands of Mr. Takata, far less wrinkled then than his own were now, but at the time he'd been struck by the grooves and lines of time on hands that moved so deftly, with such certainty among the blooms. Now as he looked at his own hands, the wrinkles seemed to belong to someone else, yet there they were. It was incredible to him, this business of being eighty-two; he was old, but not dead quite yet, as Sofía often liked to remind him when they woke up, *Well, good morning, old man, congratulations, you're not yet dead*. He was alive here in the garden, waiting. But for what? He didn't know. For the night, for whatever comes next, for the calm of dirt and vines to seep into his skin, for another question, for an answer about the North, for an answer about the South, for a map to navigate the terrors ahead, for the end of the world, for the way a leaf would still catch sunlight during the end of the world. For the frog. With a shudder, he realized he was waiting for the frog. But he won't come, he thought, that old friend of mine, he was never here on this particular land and in any case he's long gone, of course, if he ever existed at all, and so are his children and great-great-great-great-grandchildren, that's surely how it goes in a frog life, generations speed madly around the circle and there's no stopping the wheel. So many creatures come and go, are left behind; we're all crushed by time, there's no escaping it, some of us more violently than others, some eras are more violent than others, and now with the shift in global order and the coming climate horrors tell me what shape of violence is in store, what will erupt, what will collapse, what will get unleashed and what will burn to the ground, what is the next generation going to do and the generation after that, what's left of the dream we had for the world and how the hell are we going to— He put his head in his hands. Took a breath. Took the gift of oxygen into his animal lungs, exhaled to the trees, back to the green circle, the circle of air. Sometimes, when despair threatened to swallow him, Sofía would lightly punch his shoulder and say, *There you go moping again when look at what's actually all around you.* And what was around him? The gathering dark. The sigh of leaves. Zucchini, carnations, daisies. Dogs barked playfully, just out of sight. Far away, a crisis gathered its strength, like a storm cloud on the horizon, bound for everywhere. Still the earth breathed. Off-balance, too hot, too many storms, but it breathed. Buds pushed at their own casing on the rosebushes. Weeds clamored; look, he thought, at all that wild green from last week's rain.

"Hello?" he said into the warm November air. "Can you hear me?"

He laughed at himself, out loud, he couldn't help it. He was ridiculous. And so what. Here he was, once a president, a former political prisoner, and the poorest this and that, talking to the nothingness like a senile old man, or, even worse, talking to a dead frog, hoping to hear the dead frog's voice say *You're an asshole* or *Hum-de-dum* or *You barely know the ocean of the possible.* He was still laughing, and his laugh broke the air, shattered a spell that might have dragged him into sadness.

Come on, creaky old man, he muttered to himself as he rose from his chair and crouched down at the base of the tomato plant. Go on and tend what's right in front of you. The dirt offered up its fragrance. The weeds were proud, shouting bright, but if the tomatoes were to thrive the weeds would have to share the earth.

Even horror is an opening. Every moment a new beginning, until we reach the end.

So the old man thought as he dug his hands into the dirt and got to work.

Acknowledgments

I am incredibly grateful:

To my agent, Victoria Sanders, for fifteen years of support, love, advocacy, vision, and abiding belief in me. Thank you for helping me give birth to these books. To Bernadette Baker-Baughman, Jessica Spivey, and Diane Dickensheid, for their essential and tireless work on my behalf at the agency office and beyond. To my editor, Carole Baron, for all your time and brilliant insights and camaraderie, with this book and the five that came before. To the entire team at Knopf, Vintage, and Vintage Español, including Reagan Arthur, Abby Endler, Rob Shapiro, Tom Pold, Rita Madrigal, Pei Loi Koay, Susan Brown, Julie Ertl, Nick Latimer, Morgan Fenton, and Cristóbal Pera—thank you for the many, many things you do not only on behalf of my books, but for literary culture as a whole.

To San Francisco State University and the George and Judy Marcus Fund, for supporting an eight-day writing retreat on the Uruguayan coast that allowed me to capture the shape of this book. To Daniel Kochen, thank you for the hospitality. To Gabi Renzi and Zara Cañiza, my soul-sisters, for always making me feel deeply, wildly at home the instant I set foot in Uruguay, and for accompanying me so generously in research and in dreaming.

Although this book is absolutely a work of fiction, it's inspired by real-life former president of Uruguay José Mujica, aka el Pepe. My research grew many tendrils and drew on twenty years of obsessive dives taken for prior novels, but I extend particular thanks to a few key books for their exhaustive documentation: *Una oveja negra al poder: Pepe Mujica, la política de la gente,* by Andrés Danza and Ernesto Tulbovitz; *Comandante Facundo: el revolucionario Pepe Mujica,* by Walter Pernas; and *Pepe Mujica: palabras y sentires,* by Andrés Cencio. I also humbly thank José Mujica and his wife, Lucía Topolansky, for the lives they have lived and the generosity with which they've shared their voices, ideas, and stories. Thank you to the Biblioteca Nacional de Uruguay, and to the library at the University of California, Berkeley, for its excellent Latin American Studies collection. I also wish to acknowledge the countless conversations I've had over the decades with individual, ordinary Uruguayans about history, culture, and politics, from leading intellectuals and activists to friends, family, and strangers at the open-air market or on the bus or wherever conversation happens, which, in Uruguay, is everywhere. I am grateful to each and every one of these people for their contributions to my knowing and imagining.

Thank you to every one of you who has sought ways to advocate for a better, brighter world since November 2016, and also before that, reaching all the way back. Thank you for taking part in weaving the future.

Huge thanks to Chip Livingston, Gen Del Raye, Marcelo de León, and Achy Obejas, for reading early versions of the manuscript and helping it become stronger. Thank you to the various people in my family and community who sustained me, loved me, and held me in various ways while I worked on this book, including Shanna Lo Presti, Angie Cruz, Jaquira Díaz, Aya de Leon, Cristina García, Sujin Lee, Darlene Nipper, Parnaz Foroutan, Margo Edwards, and the whole cherished tribe over in Buenos Aires. Thank you to my kids, Rafael and Luciana, who show me every day what beauty means, what the world can be, and what we're fighting for. And for my wife, Pamela Harris, I have the most infinite possible gratitude, for this marriage that began when marriages like ours were still against the law, and which is built on—as we've always called it—a culture of radical support. You are the woman of my wildest dreams; twenty years in, you take my breath away. My beloved, my best friend, first reader, co-conspirator in all things: gracias. Let's grow everything here, everything we can.

A NOTE ABOUT THE AUTHOR

Carolina De Robertis is the author of five novels, including *Cantoras,* winner of a Stonewall Book Award and a Reading Women Award; a finalist for the Kirkus Prize, a Lambda Literary Award, and a California Book Award; and a *New York Times* Editors' Choice. Her work has been translated into seventeen languages, and she has received a National Endowment for the Arts Fellowship, Italy's Rhegium Julii Prize, and numerous other honors. A writer of Uruguayan origins, she teaches at San Francisco State University, and lives in Oakland, California, with her wife and two children.

A NOTE ON THE TYPE

Pierre Simon Fournier *le jeune* (1712–1768), who designed the type used in this book, was both an originator and a collector of types. His services to the art of printing were his design of letters, his creation of ornaments and initials, and his standardization of type sizes. His types are old style in character and sharply cut. In 1764 and 1766 he published his *Manuel typographique,* a treatise on the history of French types and printing, on typefounding in all its details, and on what many consider his most important contribution to typography—the measurement of type by the point system.

Typeset by Scribe
Philadelphia, Pennsylvania

Printed and bound by Berryville Graphics
Berryville, Virginia

Book design by Pei Loi Koay